The Sarafina Series

Books 1-4

by Jen Carter

JEN CARTER

The Sarafina Series by Jen Carter

Sarafina and the Mixed up Rainbow (#1)
Sarafina and the Muddy Mess (#2)
Sarafina and the Bouncy Island (#3)
Sarafina and the Bubbly Volcano (#4)
Sarafina and the Protected Pyramid (#5)
Sarafina and the Protected Pyramid (#5)
Sarafina and the Bamboozled Countryside (#6)
Sarafina and the Raging Rainforest (#7)
Sarafina and the Broken Rules (#8)

Sarafina and

the Mixed-up Rainbow

by Jen Carter

PSST! OVER HERE!

My name is Sarafina. And I'm Mother Nature's twin sister.

Most people don't know that Mother Nature has a sister. It's always been a secret, really. But I'm here to tell you the truth.

Why? Because I know that you'll believe me. I can't tell just anyone this secret, but I know I can tell you.

So here goes.

It all started a long, long time ago. When I say a long time ago, I really mean it. Even before your grandparents were born. Before your grandparent's grandparents were born. A *really* long time ago. That's when Mother Nature came to make sure all the plants and animals were growing happy and healthy. She looked after the tiniest ants, the biggest elephants, and everything in between.

And then, after she had done the best job she could, she passed her jobs down to her daughter.

It was tradition for her daughter to become the next Mother Nature.

But this last time, Mother Nature didn't have *only* one daughter. She had twin girls. Me and my sister, Aurelia.

Aurelia was always really good with the plants and animals. She knew how to help them grow. Me, on the other hand…Well, I made a lot of mistakes. I once made a whole field of sunflowers grow upside down. Yep, the flowers were underground and the roots were poking up. But that's a story for a different time.

When we were little girls, my sister and I spent most of our time playing and singing in our special garden. But then came the day when one of us had to become the next Mother Nature. Since Aurelia was so talented, she was picked. Not me. She had to go away. I stayed in the garden with my sweet fairy friend, Zoey, and my trusty doggy friend, Zander. And I haven't gotten any older since the day Aurelia left.

I've missed her so much…until now.

You see, Aurelia is sick, and I've been called to take over her job. But I can't do it alone.

I'm going to need help.

Wish me luck.

CHAPTER 1

GOODBYE GARDEN

We were being chased by a swarm of bees.

That's right, *bees*.

And it was strange, because normally the bees don't mind if my friends and I pick their flowers. Most of the time we get along with all the plants and animals, but today, when we were picking flowers, the bees were not happy.

"Run!" yelled my friend Zander.

He's a Golden Retriever, and yes, he does talk. That's one of the things I love about him.

He had been telling us to run for five minutes. I think he meant, "Run *faster*!"

"We…are…trying!" Zoey huffed.

Even though Zoey was a fairy, she wasn't a typical fairy. She was just a little smaller than me, and her wings were made of pink rose petals. They were too heavy for flying. She had to run like me, and we were both out of breath.

Neither of us was as speedy as Zander.

"Not much farther," Zander said. "Bees can't go fast for very long, I promise!"

I hoped he was right. My heart was beating so hard that I thought it would burst through my yellow dress.

Just then, a strong gust of wind blew right at us. The sound of buzzing began fading. I kept running, but I looked over my shoulder and saw the bees were gone.

"We can stop," Zoey gasped. "They gave up!"

The three of us collapsed on the grass. I closed my eyes and breathed hard.

I heard Zander say, "It was the wind. The bees were already getting tired, and then they didn't want to fight the wind."

In my head, I thought, *Thanks wind!*

When I caught my breath, I opened my eyes. My crazy, curly red hair was in my face, so I pushed it away and looked around.

We had run all the way back to our favorite garden. I smiled.

See, we live on an island far, far away from people. I don't know if it has a name. I just call it the island. And on that island, my friends and I live in a garden. The garden doesn't have a name either. I just call it the garden. It's filled with flowers of every size and color. There are trees everywhere.

I love the garden. The weather is always warm, and the air always smells like the ocean.

I was glad to be there now.

Zander laughed. Since he was born, he had been able to imitate other animals, and he liked to make his laugh sound like a dolphin. It sure was a happy sound. "That was such an adventure!" he said with another dolphin laugh.

Zoey sat up and frowned. She didn't seem to think it was as much fun as Zander did. Her eyes changed from sky blue to grassy green. That was another amazing thing about Zoey. Her eyes changed color, normally to match the plants around her.

She patted her brown hair, which had flowers weaved into it. Then she smoothed out her pink dress, which had even more flowers. It almost looked like the flowers were growing out of her dress.

"I wonder why the bees were upset," she said. "Normally they don't mind when we pick flowers."

Zander sat up on his hind legs and sniffed the air. "Actually, something is different today," he said. "Something isn't right."

He walked in a circle, looking around. He had the best eyes of any animal I knew. We've always said he had "eagle eyes." If there was something wrong around us, he would be able to spot it.

And then, it happened.

Zander said, "Uh-oh."

I sat up. It's never good when someone says *uh-oh*.

"Here comes your uncle," he continued.

I looked where Zander was looking. Just beyond the garden, at the top of the hill, was Mother Nature's castle. That's where Aurelia went when she was chosen to be the next Mother Nature. It probably has a name, but I just call it the castle. And Zander was right. My uncle was walking down the hill across the wild grass toward us.

Zoey gulped. She grabbed my arm. Her face was right next to mine, and I could smell the pretty flowers in her hair.

My uncle doesn't mean to make anyone nervous, but sometimes he does. His job is to make sure everything on Earth stays on schedule. The days and nights have to be just the right amount of time, and sometimes he has to make people hurry up. Humans call him Father Time.

Since he's my uncle, though, I just call him Uncle T.

I've heard that humans think he's old looking, but he's not. His short blond hair is always parted and combed perfectly, he doesn't have any wrinkles, and he always walks really fast.

I asked him once why people thought he looked like a great-grandpa when he really looked more like a dad. He shrugged and said he didn't have time to think about it.

I waved to him and called, "Hey Uncle T! We just escaped a swarm of bees. I hope your morning hasn't been so crazy."

He stopped a couple feet away from us and checked his wristwatch. Then he straightened his shirt and tie.

"Sarafina," he said. His voice was very serious. "I need you to come with me. Right away."

I remembered what Zander said a moment ago. *Uh-oh.* From the sounds of things, *uh-oh* was right. Uncle T didn't look like he was joking. But then again, he never really looked like he was joking.

"Is everything okay?" I asked.

Uncle T checked his wristwatch again. "I'm

sure it will be, but I need you to come with me now."

I stood up. "Can Zoey and Zander come?"

Uncle T looked at my friends. Zander was sitting like a good dog with his tongue hanging out of his mouth. Zoey was still clinging to my arm. Uncle T thought a moment. Then he nodded. "They probably should come. We could use their help."

He turned and began hiking toward the castle. We scrambled to our feet and followed.

"This must be a big deal," Zoey whispered. "You haven't been to the castle in years. Zander and I have never been there."

"Yeah," Zander whispered. "Why would he need our help?"

"Let's ask," I said. Then I looked at my uncle who was a couple steps ahead of us. "Uncle T, what's happening?"

He pointed to the castle without turning around. "Your sister is sick," he said.

I stopped walking. My friends stopped, too.
What?

My sister was sick? How could that be? Mother Nature never got sick.

"Please keep up," Uncle T said. He still hadn't turned around to look at us, but somehow he knew we had stopped. "We have no time to lose."

If Mother Nature was sick, what would happen to all the plants and animals? That's what I wanted to ask Uncle T, but I was too afraid.

Then Zander said, "Let's go find out what happened." He galloped after Uncle T. Zoey and I followed.

I looked over my shoulder for one second. *Goodbye, garden*, I thought.

If this was as serious as it seemed, we probably wouldn't be back for a long time.

CHAPTER 2

HELLO CASTLE

From my garden, the castle looked beautiful. Up close, it was even more beautiful. It was made of smooth, light pink marble with white swirls. From the front, it looked like just one tall tower. But I knew that from the inside, it looked totally different.

When Uncle T reached the castle, he touched the smooth wall. A doorway appeared for him, and he walked through. The door disappeared as soon as he was inside.

My friends and I looked at each other.

"Will a door open for you if you touch the wall, too?" Zander asked.

I shrugged. "I don't know."

I thought about the last time I was there. It

was a long time ago when Uncle T tested my talents. It was way back before I stopped growing. The memory was fuzzy, but I can say this: it didn't go well.

Suddenly, my stomach felt flip-floppy.

I stepped forward and gently touched the wall with my finger. A small, low window appeared. I crouched down and looked through it.

A moment later, I could feel Zander putting his paws on my head so he could get a good view.

"What do you see?" Zoey asked. I could hear her jumping behind us and trying to use her wings to float for a couple seconds so that she could see, too.

"Nothing," I said. "It's all dark."

"Sarafina," Uncle T called from inside. "Touch the wall with your whole hand like you mean it. Please come in and sit down."

I stood and did as he said. I pushed against the wall with my whole hand, and a doorway appeared for us.

The rose petals of Zoey's wings fluttered against my arms; Zander's fur brushed against my leg. I felt a little better knowing my friends were there with me. We all went inside.

The room we walked into was called the White Room. I remembered that. But even if I didn't remember, I could have figured it out. The room was so white that it nearly glowed. The ceiling was glass so that the morning sun shined in. The air was a little chilly inside the castle, even though it was warm outside.

In the middle of the room were four black chairs and a big black table. That was it.

The rest of the room was bare—except for three doors in a row on the far wall. I squinted at the doors, thinking. I only remembered two doors from when I was there last time. I didn't remember three.

Something seemed strange. I couldn't put my finger on it at first. Then it hit me. The room had no smell. I was so used to my garden filled with flowers and ocean breezes. This was so different. The air was chilly, the walls were bare, and there was no smell. I didn't really like it.

Uncle T sat down in a black chair. I sat down next to him, and Zoey sat next to me. Zander jumped onto the last chair. His tongue was hanging out of his mouth.

Uncle T checked his watch and then folded his hands on the table. "Sarafina," he said, "your sister became ill last night. I don't think she will be better right away."

I gulped. That was bad news.

"Now," Uncle T continued, "this has never happened before. I've watched over every Mother Nature since the beginning of time, and none have ever been sick."

I gulped again. "Will she get better? Maybe in a couple days?" I asked.

"I hope so. But until then, you have to take over her job."

My mouth dropped open. "What? I can't do that!" I shook my head. I shook it so hard that my crazy red hair got in my eyes. I shook it so fast that I started to feel dizzy. "I don't have her talent! Remember?"

Even though I was still shaking my head and feeling dizzy, I could see Uncle T checking his wristwatch. Before he could say anything, I kept talking. I couldn't stop myself.

"When we were little girls, you tested both of us," I said. "Aurelia had all the talent. I made all the mistakes. Remember the upside down flowers? The roots were growing toward the sky instead of underground!"

"You have talent," Uncle T said. "Your sister just controlled her talent more than you." He pointed to Zoey and Zander. "I wouldn't call your friends mistakes."

I looked at my friends. Then I took a deep

breath. Uncle T was right. They weren't mistakes.

When Uncle T had tested me all those years ago, he asked me to make a rose bush bloom. When I tried, a little fairy named Zoey appeared instead. Then when I helped a mommy dog have puppies, one of them made sounds like other animals and had eagle eyes. I begged to keep the fairy and the puppy, and from then on, they were my best friends.

"It's true, Feenie," Zander said. (That's what he liked to call me sometimes. *Feenie.*) "If you didn't have any talent, I wouldn't be here."

"Me neither," Zoey added. "And we love being who we are. I love my flowery hair and rose petal wings. Zander loves his dolphin laugh. It's the prettiest sound in the world."

Zander laughed. I think he just wanted to prove that Zoey was right.

"Even better," Uncle T interrupted, "Zoey and Zander have big hearts and important talents because of you. Remember what you can do and think positively. I can help you with the rest."

I shook my head like crazy again. "No," I said. "Please and *no* thank you! I really don't want the job."

Uncle T ignored me. "So we need to get started right away," he said. Then he stood up and pulled out a silver pocket watch. He looked at it and compared it to his wristwatch. "Perfect timing. Come with me."

"Wait! Uncle T?" I stood up and felt my stomach get flip-floppy again. "Can I see my sister first? I haven't seen her in so long. I'm worried about her being sick."

Uncle T shook his head. "Not now, Sarafina. She needs her rest. And I need to show you around." He paused and looked at us. "Besides," he added slowly. "It hasn't been that long. She's been with you every day." He turned and walked toward the middle door at the back of the room.

I looked at Zoey and Zander. "She's been with us every day?" I whispered to them. "What does that mean?"

My friends looked at each other and then back at me. Zoey shrugged.

"Maybe he'll tell us more," Zander said. "Let's go find out."

I nodded. We followed Uncle T to the door. It was big, black, and heavy looking. I stared at it, wondering what was on the other side.

CHAPTER 3

THE EYES OF ISLA

Uncle T reached for the door handle. Then he looked back at us.

"Each of these three doors leads to a different part of the castle," he said. With his free hand, he pointed to the door on the left. "Over there we have the Animal Kingdom. Mother Nature goes there when animals need help." He pointed to the door on the right. "Over there we have the Plant Kingdom. She goes there when plants need help."

He looked at me. "You probably remember those two parts of the castle from when you were here last time."

I nodded. "A little. I sort of remember the Animal Kingdom and the Plant Kingdom." I pointed to the middle door. "But I don't remember that one."

Uncle T turned the handle but didn't push the door open. "That's right. You didn't have permission to see this part of the castle before. Now you do."

He opened the door and stepped through.

Zander looked up at me. "Permission?" he asked.

I nodded. "We need to have Mother Nature's permission to see everything in the castle. That's why humans can't see the castle at all. They don't have permission. We only see what we're allowed to see."

I remembered *that*. It made me wonder what else was hidden in the castle.

Zoey patted my arm. "Let's go in," she whispered. "Let's find out what's in there."

In the middle of the room was a throne made of sparkling silver. It was so sparkly I had to squint at first. When my eyes got used to it, I couldn't believe what I saw. Yes, the throne was beautiful and sparkly, but that wasn't the only interesting thing about it. A big, all-white peacock sat on one of its arms. She looked at us, and then she hopped to the middle of her throne and fanned her white feathers behind her like a lacy curtain.

"Wow," Zoey said.

I wanted to say the same thing.

Wow.

But instead of saying *wow*, I looked at Uncle T standing next to the door and asked, "Uncle T, what is this place?"

"This is where you will go to check on the Elements."

"What are the Elements?" I asked.

Uncle T held up a finger as he said the name of each Element slowly. "Air, Fire, Earth, and Water."

I closed my eyes and shook my head.

"Why would I need to check on Air and Fire…and what were the others again?"

"Earth and Water." Uncle T looked at his wristwatch. "Because you have to keep them under control. You know how wild they can get. Come along." He started walking toward the peacock.

I gasped. And then I screeched, "What? Control Fire? Control Water? I can't do that!"

"Sarafina, don't be dramatic," Uncle T said. "There isn't time to be dramatic."

"Don't worry," Zander said. "We'll help you."

I leaned down and scratched the top of his head. He was so brave. Unfortunately, I did *not* feel brave.

Zoey took my hand and led me toward the peacock's throne. "Let's go see," she said softly. Zander followed.

"This is Isla," Uncle T said.

I gave Uncle T a confused look. I had never heard a name like that before. "What's her name again?" I asked.

"Isla," he said. "Like *eye-la*."

I nodded. Sounds like *eye-la*, I told myself. Got it.

I studied Isla as we stopped a couple feet away. The feathers on her head reminded me of a tiara. And her blue eyes looked so familiar. I felt like I had seen her before.

How strange. Why did she seem so familiar?

Uncle T cleared his throat. "The circle at the end of each feather is like a video camera. When you touch it, a picture of a different part of the world will appear. This is how you will keep track of the Elements."

I scrunched my eyebrows. Uncle T was acting crazy again. Video camera feathers? How did that work?

He reached toward one feather. "See here?" At his touch, the feather came to life, and a picture appeared on it. "Here's your garden. We can see

25

that the Element *Air* is making a nice breeze blow gently through the trees. Sometimes Air can get carried away, but he's behaving right now."

I could see it—I could see our garden in the peacock feather. The trees were rustling in the breeze.

"Wow," I breathed. I was amazed. And a little homesick, too. Then I thought about how that strong gust of wind stopped the bees from chasing us earlier. I wondered if that was the Element Air at work.

Uncle T continued, "You can touch a feather and see anywhere in the world. But also, if an Element is misbehaving, Isla will tell you. A feather will light up and show you a picture of the problem. That way, you'll know that you're needed."

He pointed past Isla's throne. "See the door there? Once the feather shows you the problem, just unlock the door. It will lead you wherever you need to go."

I was about to ask how to unlock the door when Uncle T held up a ring of keys. He handed them to me. They were cold like metal, and each was a different color.

"Don't lose those," he said. "Keep them safe. If you aren't in Isla's room when the Elements need you, the keys will buzz. That will let you know it's time to get to work."

"Here!" Zoey said. She held out her hand for the keys. "I'll tie them onto your belt for you."

I handed the keys to her and watched as she tied them onto the belt of my yellow dress.

"Uncle T, I don't know how to control anything," I said. "I definitely can't control Air or those other things you were talking about."

"Air, Earth, Water, and Fire," he corrected me.

"See?" I threw up my hands. "I can't even remember their names."

"Don't get worked up, Sarafina. Your sister has done it for the last two hundred years. You have the same powers as her."

"But I haven't been practicing!"

"Zoey and Zander are here to help you."

"That's right!" Zander said. He jumped up and licked my cheek. It made me feel better. But not much better.

"In fact," Uncle T said, I'm going to show them their jobs right now. You stay here and get to know Isla."

I looked at my friends. Then I looked at my uncle. "Can I please see my sister?" I asked.

Uncle T shook his head. "Not now. Soon. But not now." He motioned for Zoey and Zander to follow him.

"Wait!" I called as they walked away. "I can't do this. I'm too afraid."

Uncle T pursed his lips and nodded. He was thinking.

"You will need to be brave and overcome your fear," he said simply. "The world depends on it."

Then he led my friends out of the room.

As they walked away, Zoey turned and gave me a half-smile. She mouthed, "You can do it."

I didn't really believe her.

CHAPTER 4

AIRY AIR

I gulped. I was alone—except for that peacock, of course. So I did the only thing I could. I walked over to Isla and asked her, "So, do you talk?"

She stared at me. She tilted her head to one side.

"Okay, I guess the answer is no." I crossed my arms and squinted at her. "Do I know you? I feel like I know you somehow."

Again, Isla didn't answer.

I looked around. The walls were just as white and bare as they were in the White Room.

"What do I do now?" I asked. "Do I just wait for a feather to light up? Can I ever leave this room, or do I have to live here?"

I hadn't thought about that before. Did I have

to *live* there? Could I ever go back to the garden?

This day was getting worse by the second.

Just then, one of Isla's feathers began to glow. I gasped and leaned toward it. In its glowing circle, I could see a desert. Wind was blowing sand around in a terrible way.

"It's a sandstorm!" I said. My heart started beating quickly. "What do I do?"

Isla turned her head. It seemed like she was trying to look behind her.

"Oh, the door!" I exclaimed. I rushed past Isla's throne to the door. I fumbled with the keys that Zoey had put on my belt.

"Which one? Which ONE!?!"

I didn't have time to untie the keys. I tried sticking each one in the keyhole while still on my belt. Oh, how silly I must have looked! Finally the yellow one fit.

The door swung open. In front of me a white marble staircase spiraled upward. It seemed to go on and on. I couldn't see the top.

But it didn't matter how tall it was. I had to go no matter what. I took a deep breath, and then I raced upward, taking two steps at a time.

Before I knew it, I could see where it ended, high in the sky. And I was almost there. Running up the stairs went much faster than I thought, and

I didn't even get out of breath.

I stepped onto a platform at the top of the staircase and peered over the side. Down below was the desert I had seen on Isla's feather. Sand flew *everywhere*, but none of it touched me. There must have been an invisible barrier protecting me.

Then I heard a voice.

"Hey!" it said in a loud whisper. "You're not Mother Nature. Who are you? What are you doing up here?"

I spun around. No one was there.

"What's happening?" I asked aloud. "Who are you? Where are you?"

Sand blasted against the invisible wall. I flinched.

"It's me, *Air*! I'm one of the four mighty Elements, of course! And I'm talking to you, silly girl. Hey, I know who you are now. You must be Mother Nature's sister. You look a lot like her. You both have the same blue eyes and fluffy red hair. I always thought that fluffy hair was perfect for a breeze to blow through!"

More sand blasted against the invisible wall. This time, I tried not to flinch.

"I didn't know that you were real," Air said. "I heard rumors that Mother Nature had a sister, but I didn't know for sure. So glad to meet ya! Let me see, do I remember your name? Sarafina, right? I'd shake your hand if I could, but I can't. I'm just made of air, after all."

I spun around again. Sand was blowing everywhere—just everywhere! And it was so strange hearing a voice without a body. I didn't know what to do with myself.

Okay, I thought. *I'm supposed to calm Air down. He's causing this sandstorm, and I have to make it stop. How do I do that?*

"I know, I know," Air said. "You want me to settle down. Is that right? Is that why Isla told on me? She never wants me to have any fun. But shouldn't I be allowed to have a little fun? It's only the desert. No one is even here right now. I thought it would be fun to redecorate. You know, maybe move a little sand here and there. See if I can dig up buried treasure—that kind of thing. I'm sure you understand, right?"

I smiled. Air was kind of funny.

I put my hands on my hips and looked around. "Actually, I really like what you've done with the place." I pointed to a mountain of sand off to the left. "I don't remember seeing that sand dune in Isla's feather a couple minutes ago. I bet when the sun starts to set, it's going to be even more beautiful. All these mountains of sand—it's so much more interesting than flat desert."

"I know! Those are my thoughts exactly," Air said.

"I hope you don't want to redecorate too much more. We should have some time to enjoy this."

Suddenly, the sand stopped flying around. It settled to the ground.

"Really?" Air asked. "But who will enjoy it? No one is here."

I bit my lip. He was right—no one was there. But I had to come up with something to say.

"The sun!" I said. "I think the sun would love for these sandy mountains to be the last thing he sees before going to sleep."

"*Hmm*," Air said. "The sun has always liked my landscape artwork. I bet he *does* like the way the desert looks now."

"Absolutely," I said. "This could be like a present to him."

Air was silent for a moment. "I have always liked the sun. I hope he knows that."

"I bet a nice present would let him know."

"Hey, I like you, Mother Nature's sister. And I'll do it. I'll give the sun a present of a beautiful desert landscape."

"Great!" I said.

"I'm going to tell the sun right now that I have a present for him."

"Perfect!"

"Well, see ya later, Mother Nature's sister. Nice to meet you!"

I smiled. "You too," I said.

And I really meant it. Air was funny.

"Oh, but before you go," he said, "is your sister all right?"

My smile faded. I shrugged. "I don't know. She's sick."

A burst of sand flew at the invisible wall one more time. "When you see her, blow her a kiss from me!"

I tried to smile again, but it was harder now that I was thinking about Aurelia.

"I will," I said.

CHAPTER 5

THE PURSE OF POWER

My friends and Uncle T were waiting in Isla's room when I got back.

"Feenie!" Zander exclaimed as he galloped to me. He jumped up and put his paws on my shoulders. "Where were you?" he asked.

I laughed. It was funny looking at Zander face-to-face. Sometimes I think he forgets that he's a dog.

"I had to go talk to Air," I said with a smile. "He was causing a big sandstorm."

Uncle T's eyebrows arched upward. "Did you get him to stop?"

I thought about my meeting with Air.

"I think so," I said. "He said he was going to stop. But…" I couldn't exactly say what I was thinking about Air. It was hard to put into words.

"He seems wishy-washy, right?" Uncle T said.

"Exactly!" My eyes grew. "I think he could change his mind."

Uncle T shook his head. "That's Air for you." He checked his wristwatch. "Come along, you three. We need to do some talking."

He turned toward the door, and we followed him back to the White Room.

On the black table was a silvery purse. As Uncle T sat down at the table, he pointed at it.

"This here is Mother Nature's," he said. "She keeps all her tools in it."

"Tools?" I asked. My friends and I sat down at the table. We leaned toward the purse.

Uncle T nodded. "Mostly you will just need to use your mind and concentrate to use your Mother Nature talents. But sometimes you might need a little help from these tools." He opened the purse and started pulling things out. "Mirror, phone, perfume, money—" he paused, squinting into the purse "—and a lot of makeup."

"Those are her *tools*?" Zoey asked.

"Yes," Uncle T answered. "All these things help Mother Nature fix problems, heal animals and plants, and control the Elements. The tools are disguised, though. If the purse was ever lost around humans, Mother Nature would want it to seem like a regular old purse with regular old stuff inside."

I looked at my friends.

"Mother Nature sure is smart," Zander said.

That's exactly what I was thinking. I wanted to say *way smarter than me*, but I didn't.

Some of the tools seemed familiar. As I studied them, I felt like I should have remembered them from when Uncle T tested me long ago. The little bottle of brown liquid—was it makeup or was it paint? I seemed to remember brown paint that changed colors. And the coins—did they... *talk*? The memory was foggy. It felt more like a dream.

"How do the tools work?" I asked.

Uncle T shrugged. "Good question. I don't know exactly. That's something only Mother Nature knows. But I'm sure you will figure it out."

I shook my head and squeezed my eyes shut. I wanted to ask what would happen if I couldn't figure it out.

Uncle T packed up the purse and pushed it across the table to me. He was ignoring my head shaking.

"Hang onto this," he said. "You can pull on

the handles to turn them into a long strap if you like."

I kept shaking my head. "I'm always losing things," I said. "I'm afraid I'll lose this, too."

"I'll hold it," Zoey said. She smiled. "It's so pretty, and it will go perfectly with my pink dress."

I handed her the purse. She pulled on the handles to make them long. Then she put the strap over her head so that it crossed her chest.

"Now," Uncle T said. "I'd like to tell you a little more about the Elements. You've met Air, but he's not the only one you have to watch over—"

Before Uncle T could finish, an alarm sounded. He looked at his pocket watch and pressed a button so that it stopped ringing.

"We will have to finish this later," he said. "I have to go to a meeting." He stood and nodded at us. "You can stay here. I'll be back soon."

He disappeared through Isla's door.

"I wonder where he's going," Zander said.

I nodded. "Me too," I said. "And I wonder what he was going to say about the other Elements." My shoulders dropped. I was disappointed that I didn't get to hear what he was going to say.

"How are you feeling, Feenie?" Zoey asked.

"Are you okay? This has been a crazy morning."

She was right. It was crazy. Crazier than the time I accidentally gave dragonfly wings to ladybugs and then gave ladybug shells to dragonflies.

"Do you need to rest?" Zander asked. "Maybe we can go back to the garden for a little while."

My shoulders slumped. "I just want to see my sister."

Zoey and Zander looked at each other. Then Zoey said slowly, "I think we have to wait for that. But maybe we can show you something interesting while we wait."

I perked up. "Like what?"

Zoey and Zander looked at each other again. Then they got up from the table.

"Follow us," Zander said as he pranced toward the three doors at the back of the White Room.

CHAPTER 6

TREES AND BUBBLES, REALLY?

My friends went straight for the door on the right. Zoey reached for the handle and smiled. "It's been a long time since you've seen the Plant Kingdom. Remember this?" She opened the door.

The Plant Kingdom smelled like our garden back home. There was grass covering the ground for as far as I could see. It looked like we had just stepped onto a big field surrounded by blue sky and sunshine. In front of us were seven big trees. Each tree was different. One was short and thick with big, dark leaves. Another was tall and thin with long, bare branches. Every one of them had different traits.

Zoey fluttered her wings and skipped toward the trees. Her eyes turned green to match the grass.

"Isn't it beautiful?" she asked. She spun around.

I nodded. I remembered the trees, but just barely. I hadn't been there for a long time.

"Did Uncle T show you this while I was talking to Air?" I asked.

Zoey and Zander both nodded.

"I can't remember what the trees do," I said. "Remind me?"

Zoey spun around one more time. Then she galloped back to Zander and me. "Each tree will take you to a different continent on Earth."

"How?" I asked.

Zoey pointed to the key ring on my belt.

"First, the green key will buzz. That will let you know we need to come here to the Plant Kingdom. Then we'll use the trees." She pointed to a smooth, fat tree with light green leaves. "See that? There is a door in each tree trunk, and the door we need will open. We'll go into the tree, and it will take us where we need to go."

"Should we try it out now?" I asked. I didn't remember tree transporters, but they sounded like fun.

"No way!" Zander said. "I want to show you the Animal Kingdom, too!" He jumped around in a happy circle.

We turned around and left the Plant Kingdom. We were only back in the White Room for a second—just long enough to take a deep breath. Then Zoey opened the door to the Animal Kingdom.

Zander said, "If you don't really remember this one either, just wait. You'll *love* this!"

The Animal Kingdom looked a lot like the Plant Kingdom with the green field and blue sky. But there weren't any trees. Instead, there were twelve enormous bubbles slowly bouncing up and down. They were probably ten feet tall. Each bubble had a different scene pictured in it from a different part of the world.

"The bubbles show different *climates*," Zander said. He lifted his nose toward a bubble that just touched the ground and bounced up. "See that one over there with all the snow? That's the ice cap climate. If we go there, we will see animals that live in that climate—like polar bears."

My mouth dropped open and my eyes grew. I didn't remember this at all. Did Mother Nature change the way the Kingdoms worked? This was really cool.

"And look over there." Zander turned his nose toward another bubble. "See that one? See those

grassy mountains? That's the highland climate—
like the mountains. Get it? Mountains are *high,* so
they are the *high*lands. If we go there, we'll see the
animals that live there."

"So," I said slowly, "how do we know which
place we are supposed to visit? And how do we
use these…um…bubbles?"

"The one we need will come to us," Zander
said. "It just takes a minute. These bubbles travel
slowly."

"Let's go somewhere," I said.

Before Zoey or Zander could answer, I felt the
key ring on my belt start vibrating.

"Uh-oh," I said. I looked down at the keys.
The yellow one was buzzing. "It looks like Air is
calling us."

"Let's go!" Zoey said.

We left the Animal Kingdom and rushed
through the White Room toward Isla's Element
room. Two seconds later, Uncle T appeared
behind us.

How did he know we were called? I had the
keys, not him. I wondered if he had a set of his
own keys.

I was just about to ask when Zoey said,
"Look!"

One of Isla's feathers was glowing.

My friends and I scurried closer. Soon I could see the picture in the feather. It was a storm over a city. A rainbow was flashing on and off in the sky.

"What's happening?" Zander asked.

"Oh boy," Uncle T said from behind.

My friends and I turned toward him.

Uncle T took a deep breath. "It looks like Air is playing games with the sun and the rain. The storm is clearing up, but Air is making it difficult for the rainbow to appear."

We looked back at Isla's glowing feather. The rainbow continued blinking in the sky.

"That's so strange," Zoey said. "I've never seen anything like that."

"What do we need to do, Uncle T?" I asked.

"Make Air stop. No time to talk now. Just go!"

I scrambled to the door. Zander and Zoey were right behind me.

"This sure has been a busy morning!" Zander said.

"And it's about to get even busier!" Zoey added.

They were definitely right.

CHAPTER 7

AIR'S NOT-SO-FUNNY TRICK

Finally, I found the yellow key on my belt and unlocked the door. Just as I swung it open, I heard Uncle T's voice behind us.

"Remember to use Mother Nature's purse!" he called.

"Got it!" Zoey called back. She patted the strap across her chest.

Then we ran up the marble staircase. I led the way. Zoey and Zander were right behind me.

When we got to the top, everything looked different. Last time when I peered over the side of the platform, I saw the desert. This time I saw a neighborhood. There were houses everywhere. Some cars were parked on the street. In the middle of all the houses, there was a school. I could see the playground and field not too far from the classrooms. In the sky, the rainbow continued to flicker.

"Where are we?" Zander asked.

"I'm not sure," I said. "But I hope kids aren't in school right now."

Out of the corner of my eye, I could see Zoey nodding.

I took a deep breath. Somehow, I knew I had to be stern with Air. I just wasn't sure if I could be.

"Air!" I called. "What are you up to? We know it's you!"

The rain was flying in all directions around us—not just down to the ground. It splattered sideways against the invisible wall around the platform. It even seemed like rain was hitting the bottom of the platform, almost like it was falling upward rather than down.

A voice filled the sky, but it wasn't Air's voice. It was a girl's voice.

"Oh, he's at it again," the voice said. "Air is always playing games. The sun is trying to break through the clouds, and Air is being difficult." The voice sounded like it was taking a deep breath. "Air, give us a break, please! Stop pushing the clouds around. Sun wants to get through!"

Whose voice was that? It wasn't Air…it had to be a different Element…

Water! It was raining, so that voice must have been Water's voice!

"Water?" I said loudly. "Is that you?"

Before the girl's voice could answer, I heard Air.

"Well," he said, "I am quite sad about Mother Nature being sick. Of course I like you plenty, Sarafina, but still I'm worried about your sister. I thought we could show her how much we care by doing something unique—like making a blinking rainbow!"

"What's going on?" Zoey asked.

I thought really hard. How were rainbows made? I had to know the answer to that. *I had to!* It was just hard to remember.

"I know," I whispered to myself. "Rainbows are made when the sun shines through the rain at just the right angle." How was Air making the rainbow blink?

It only took a second, and then it came to me. I turned to my friends.

"Every time the sun breaks through the clouds and the rainbow forms, Air pushes more clouds in front of it. That's why the rainbow looks like it's blinking. He's basically turning the rainbow on and off." I pointed to the clouds. "Look at how he has shaped the clouds into tall, skinny strips and is moving them fast past the sun."

Zoey started digging through Mother Nature's purse. "Zander!" she said. "Come help me. Maybe we can find something in here that will help. Sarafina, try using your Mother Nature talent. See if you can push all the clouds away."

"Yes!" Zander said as he bounced over to Zoey. "Overpower Air!"

I took a deep breath. I hadn't tried using my Mother Nature talent since the time I gave zebras polka dots instead of stripes. But moving clouds had to be easier than that, right?

I closed my eyes and concentrated on pushing all the clouds away.

Rain continued to pound against the platform from every direction. The noise made concentrating hard. Nothing was happening.

"Oh, good try, Sarafina," Air said. "If I had hands, I would clap!" A strong gust of wind slammed against the platform. "But silly girl, you can't do anything with that invisible wall around you!" He laughed.

Zander growled. "How do we get it to go away, then?" he asked, baring his teeth.

"Ask nicely!" Air sang. "If you ask nicely, I

might tell you!"

"Oh, Air, leave them alone." It was the girl's voice again. "Stop teasing everyone so much." She sighed. "Young lady, just *ask* for the wall to come down. That's all you have to do. Hurry, though. I'm almost done raining. And be careful. You're going to get really wet—really fast."

So it *was* Water's voice! She just said she was raining—that had to be Water then.

"And watch your balance," Air added. "My winds have been known to knock people over from time to time!"

I closed my eyes again, but this time I wasn't concentrating on the clouds. This time I simply said to myself, *Please take this invisible wall down. Thank you!*

Zoey and Zander had stopped looking through the purse. I could feel Zoey squeezing my arm and Zander nuzzling against my leg to encourage me.

Please take this invisible wall down, I thought again. *Please and thank you!*

Suddenly, water was splashing all over us. *Very* cold water was splashing all over us. I never really thought about how cold water would be this high in the sky, but there was no question about it. It was *cold!*

"Okay, now try!" Zoey said. She scrunched her eyes shut and spit water out. Her flowery hair was drooping and drenched, but she pushed it over her shoulders and tried to shield us from the rain with her wings. They weren't quite big enough to act as an umbrella, but she tried anyway.

"Here goes nothing!" I said, also spitting water out. I closed my eyes and pushed my arms out in front of me as though I was pushing the clouds away. I knew it might sound crazy, but I even blew a hard breath out. Maybe I could blow the clouds away. It was worth a try.

Clouds, go away, I said to myself. *Go away, go away! Don't listen to Air anymore!*

I tried pushing my arms from side to side. Maybe I could direct the clouds the way humans sometimes directed traffic.

"You're doing great," Zander said. "Keep going!"

And then it happened. The platform began to warm up. Rain continued to splatter us, but it was no longer so cold, and it no longer stung. It felt soft, in fact. It even felt, well, *colorful.*

"Look!" Zoey exclaimed. "Look at this!"

I had been concentrating so hard that it took a moment for me to realize Zoey was talking.

I opened my eyes.

We were surrounded by colors—every shade of color from red to violet. The colors danced around like warm, wet drops of happiness. And there were butterflies everywhere. Just everywhere!

What had happened?

"You did it, Feenie!" Zander said, jumping up to lick my face. "You did it! The rainbow isn't flickering anymore. The clouds are gone, and the rainbow is here to stay!"

"Hooray!" Zoey yelled. "And look—we're *in* the rainbow right now." She hugged me. "I've never been in a rainbow before."

I took a deep breath filled with relief as the butterflies all started to fly away. My wet hair was stuck to my cheeks and forehead, and my heart was thudding in my chest, but I barely noticed.

We did it, I said to myself. *We did it.*

I smiled. It was pretty cool being inside a rainbow. I had never seen so many colors in my life.

Wind swooshed across the platform, and Air laughed.

"That's right, Sarafina, you did it! You did it!" He laughed again. "But look around. Your rainbow's colors aren't in the right order!"

CHAPTER 8

THE MIXED-UP RAINBOW

I couldn't believe what Air was saying. A mixed-up rainbow? Was that even possible? I only meant to move the clouds. I didn't mean to move rainbow colors. I blinked hard and looked at the colors swirling around us.

Oh no, I thought. *Air is right!*

Red, blue, purple, orange—the colors weren't right at all.

Yikes!

Double yikes!

I should have known when the butterflies popped out of the rainbow that something was wrong. I slapped my forehead.

"You know what Mother Nature always says to me?" Air asked. He paused to blow a strong gust of wind at us. When he continued talking, it was in a high-pitched voice. *"Now Air, it's one thing to fly about and turn things upside down where there aren't any people or animals to bother. But don't go causing problems in cities. We don't want to cause a stir."* He made an 'ahem' sound and went back to his regular voice. "Just wait till she hears what *you* did here, right over a school of all places. You better fix this before recess starts!"

"Oh, Air," Water said. She made a *tsk-tsk* sound. "Your games just aren't funny. I'm going to put an end to this right now. I'll stop the shower and save the rest of the rain for next time."

I suddenly felt hot from the inside out. The water in the rainbow was warm, but that's not why I felt such heat. I was embarrassed. And I knew I could fix this. I knew I had to fix this.

"No, Miss Water, please don't!" I said. "I have to learn how to do this on my own. My sister is counting on me." I turned and looked at Zoey as a final butterfly flew away. "What did you find in Mother Nature's purse?"

Zoey began digging through it again. She threw items out of the purse one at a time, and Zander caught them in his mouth. He dropped each to the floor before Zoey threw the next one.

"How about a comb?" she asked. "A phone? Some coins? Oh, what's this?" Zoey pulled out the little bottle filled with brown liquid. "Is this makeup? I think humans use this on their faces."

In a flash, I knew what to do. That little bottle of brown makeup *was* a special kind of paint that changed colors. It all came back to me. I had used that paint when Uncle T had tested my Mother Nature talents. Now I remembered what it was for.

"Perfect!" I said. I held out my hand. "I can use that!"

Zander dropped the money that he had just caught in his mouth. "What is it?" he asked.

I twisted off the cap. "I think when nature gets confused and strange things start happening, sometimes you have to show it what to do. Aurelia used this when I mixed up the dragonfly wings and ladybug shells. If I paint a rainbow, the mixed-up one will get the idea. Then it'll fix itself." I tried to push some wet hair away from my eyes, but the warm cloud of swirly rainbow colors seemed to hold it in place. "I'm going to need help. I have nowhere to paint a rainbow!"

"On me!" Zoey said. "Paint it on my wings!"

I didn't waste a moment to think twice—I turned the bottle over and poured the liquid into my hand.

I have the greatest friends ever, I thought. *Not just anyone would help me un-mix-up a rainbow.*

The second the paint touched my hand, it turned red. It felt like jelly with lots of bubbles popping in it. It almost made my hands tingle. It was *so* tickly.

Zoey turned around and spread her wing out. The pale pink rose petals were drenched by the rain. I hoped the paint would stick.

"Red," I called as I swiped the paint across the top of Zoey's wings, "you come over here."

All around us, I could feel the colors of the mixed-up rainbow moving. The red rose above our heads.

"It's working!" Zander said.

"Orange," I said, "you're next." I poured more liquid into my hand, and this time it was orange. I spread it across Zoey's wings, right under the red arc.

Again I could feel the air shifting and changing around us. Orange found its place under red.

I kept going. Yellow came after orange, then it was green's turn, then blue, then indigo, and then violet.

Once all the colors were in place, I took a step back and looked at Zoey's wings. It looked right.

And the colors all around us felt right, too.

"Aha!" Air said with a sudden gust. "You did it. Sarafina, really, you're already surprising me with your talents. Mother Nature sure must be happy that you're her sister!"

I felt a little dizzy, and I barely heard Air's words. I was just happy that the rainbow colors were back in place.

"And with that," Water said, "the rain shower comes to an end." She sighed.

Drops stopped falling. Moments later, the rainbow faded away.

My friends and I smiled at each other. Then something else caught Zander's eye.

"Look," he said. He walked over to the side of the platform.

Below us, in a classroom window, there was a row of kids looking outside. Their eyes were wide, and they were pointing to the sky.

"Can they see us?" Zoey asked.

"I have no idea," I said, "but let's not wait to find out!"

We scrambled across the platform and back down the stairs toward the castle.

I probably should have been worried about whether those kids saw us—or saw the mixed-up rainbow. But all I could think about was my friends. I was so lucky to have all their help.

CHAPTER 9

MOTHER NATURE'S ROOM

Uncle T was waiting for us in Isla's Element room. He looked worried. His eyebrows were scrunched, and he was pacing back and forth. When he saw us, he looked excited for a moment. Then he looked worried again.

"My goodness!" he exclaimed. "What happened to you? Why are you all wet?"

I was so tired that I didn't feel much like answering. I looked at Zoey and Zander. The flowers on Zoey's dress drooped and some of her wet hair was stuck to her cheeks. Zander's golden fur dripped in a puddle all around him. He looked extra-skinny now that his fur wasn't dry and fluffy. My friends didn't look like they wanted to answer Uncle T's question either.

"We had to take the walls around the platform down to fix the rainbow," I said in a quiet voice.

"How—? Why—?" Uncle T shook his head. "Oh, it doesn't matter. If you fixed it, that's all that matters."

We nodded. I didn't say anything about the kids in the school looking out the window. I was hoping that didn't matter either.

Uncle T grabbed the end of his necktie and looked at it. I hadn't noticed before, but a clock was pictured on the tie. That's what Uncle T was studying—the clock.

He sure did have clocks everywhere.

"Well, it's time to go see Mother Nature. She's been asking about you."

I looked at my friends. My stomach flipped and flopped. I wanted to see my sister, but I was a little scared. I was so worried about how sick she was.

"Come along," Uncle T said. "Zoey and Zander, you come too. Mother Nature would like to see you as well." He turned and walked through the door. We followed him into the White Room.

"Where is she?" I asked.

"She's…" Uncle T's voice trailed off as he scratched his head. "It's hard to explain. Let me show you."

He stopped in the middle of the room where the black table and chairs were. Then he pointed at the ceiling.

"Look up."

We looked up. At first, I couldn't see anything. The castle ceiling was high, high above us, and it looked like there was nothing but a giant skylight letting the sunshine in.

"Concentrate," Uncle T said. "Think about seeing Mother Nature."

Concentrate on seeing Mother Nature?

I wanted to ask what that meant. Should I make a wish? Should I imagine my sister in my head?

But before I could ask, an image began to appear across the high ceiling. Green grass, colorful flowers, big shady trees—it looked so familiar. *So* familiar.

"It's our garden!" Zoey said.

"There's our favorite tree!" Zander added. "And look—that's where we were this morning when the bees stopped chasing us!"

"Wow," I breathed. Then I looked at Uncle T. "What's happening? Why is the garden on the castle ceiling?"

"That's where Mother Nature lives," he answered. "Her room is at the top of the castle.

We can only see it if she invites us to come in. Just a couple moments ago, she gave you permission to see her room."

"How do we get up there?" I asked.

Uncle T was still looking up. "After you practice enough, you'll just have to think about it, and you'll be there. The more you practice using your mind to do things and take you places, the easier it will become. But in the meantime, we'll do it the old fashioned way."

He tapped on the black table with his pointer finger, and it sank into the ground.

"Wow!" Zoey and Zander exclaimed.

"Step on," Uncle T said. He took a spot on the table.

We did the same.

"Up!" Uncle T commanded.

Slowly, the table began rising, rising, rising. It was like an elevator going to the top of the castle tower.

As we neared the garden scene, my friends and I ducked down. We didn't want to hit our heads.

"Don't worry," Uncle T said. "You'll go right through. You won't even feel it."

He was right. We floated through the grass and the flowers. Everything was green for a moment.

Are we inside the grass? I wondered. It smelled

like we were in the grass. And then before I knew it, everything became clear again. The table stopped moving just as our feet appeared through the grass and flowers.

It really looked like we were back in our garden. My favorite tree with the purple flowers was close enough to touch. Off in the distance I could see the ocean. The air suddenly smelled salty. I felt like I had come home.

"Are we still in the castle, really?" Zander asked. "It doesn't feel like we are in the castle."

I turned to my uncle. "Where's my sister?"

"Keep concentrating on her," he said. Then he pointed toward a tree with big, white flowers. "Concentrate on that spot right there."

We looked at the tree silently, trying to do just what Uncle T said. Slowly, something began to appear. Red hair, blue eyes...it was Mother Nature, siting against the tree.

"Aurelia!" I exclaimed. I ran to my sister's side. "Aurelia! Oh, I've missed you so much!"

I knelt down next to her and wrapped my arms around her neck.

"Are you okay?" I asked. "Aurelia, what's wrong? Are you all right?"

She gave a weak smile and patted my arms.

"I'm better now that you are here," she said.

CHAPTER 10

AURELIA

"I'll give you some time to chat," Uncle T said. He checked the pocket watch. Then he disappeared back down through the grass.

"Aurelia, where are we?" I asked. "Are we still in the castle or in the garden? I don't really understand."

My sister dropped her arms from my hug.

"This is my room in the castle. Each time a new Mother Nature takes over, she gets to decorate however she wants. I wanted my room to look like the garden where we grew up—so that I could be near you."

I shook my head. I still didn't understand. Then I remembered what Uncle T had said earlier about Aurelia being with us every day.

Slowly, I asked, "Does that mean when Zoey, Zander, and I are in the garden—in real life—that you see us here in your room?"

Mother Nature nodded. "You don't see me, but I get to be with you whenever I'm here."

That made me feel happy and sad at the same time. I was happy that my sister decorated her room like the garden, but I wished that I had known she was with us all that time.

I was also sad that my sister was so pale and worn out. Her eyes had purple circles around them, and her cheeks were sunken in. She looked older than me. She must have kept getting older when she became Mother Nature while I stayed the same. I didn't know that.

"You did a great job helping today," Aurelia said. She looked at Zoey and Zander. "And I mean all of you. You're a great team."

Zoey and Zander couldn't help themselves. They both wiggled past me to give Mother Nature a hug. Zoey wrapped her arms around Aurelia's neck, and Zander licked her cheek.

Mother Nature smiled.

"I made some mistakes," I said softly. "I mixed up a rainbow pretty badly. Some children might have even seen it."

Aurelia nodded slowly. Then she shrugged.

"It's okay for children to know some of nature's secrets. It'll be okay." She smiled, just a little. "As for the mixed-up rainbow, nothing is perfect. But nothing is a mistake either, Sarafina."

My eyebrows rose. "What do you mean?"

"I mean that sometimes things don't go as we expect. But that doesn't mean they're wrong." She lifted her hands toward Zoey and Zander. "Look at your two beautiful friends here. Dogs don't normally laugh like dolphins or have the eyesight of eagles. But isn't it wonderful that Zander does? And just wait—that's not the end of his talents."

Aurelia turned to Zoey. "And sweet Zoey here: she's a fairy who has flowers sprouting out of her hair and clothes. Have we ever had a creature like this before?" She shook her head. "But those flower petal wings are powerful. Just wait until you see what she can do when she dances." Mother Nature's eyes almost twinkled at the thought.

My friends and I looked at each other.

"Sarafina," Aurelia continued, "we are the first set of twins ever born to a Mother Nature. As Uncle T probably told you, we both have the powers of Mother Nature, but I was able to control mine a little easier than you. That's why I ended up taking the job. But I wouldn't be able to do so much of this without you."

"What do you mean?" I asked. I squinted at my sister.

Aurelia thought for a moment. "Well, for starters, have you ever seen a white peacock like Isla?"

I shook my head. Zoey and Zander shook theirs.

"When Uncle T was testing our abilities all those years ago, you created Isla. She didn't look like most peacocks, but she's special—and she gave us a new way to keep up with the Elements. Before that—" Aurelia paused and shook her head "—it was much harder."

That's why Isla looked so familiar! I knew that I had seen her before. But *I* created her? Could that be? We had done so many tests as children. I didn't remember—it was all a blur.

"Just wait," Aurelia said. "You'll see more and more that you've got talent in ways you don't expect."

"Are you going to get better?" I asked suddenly. "I don't like that you're sick. How can I help you get better?"

Aurelia shook her head. "I don't know, Sarafina."

She didn't say anything for a moment. When she spoke again, her voice sounded sad. "A

Mother Nature has never been sick before. Uncle T and I don't know what is happening."

I could feel Zoey and Zander at my sides. Zoey slipped her arm through mine. Zander stuck his head under my other hand. With them, I suddenly felt stronger. And determined.

"We are going to figure this out," I said. "Zoey, Zander, and I—we'll figure it out. Don't worry, Aurelia. We're going to take care of your jobs, and we're going to find a cure for whatever is making you sick."

Mother Nature smiled again, weakly. "Thank you, my wonderful sister." She closed her eyes.

"We better let you rest," I said. "You look tired."

Aurelia nodded. She didn't open her eyes.

With that, my friends and I walked back to the table elevator.

"Oh, Sarafina?" Aurelia called.

I looked across the garden at her. "Yes?"

"I forgot. The rainbow on Zoey's wings is lovely, but I'm sure she doesn't want it forever. When you get to the bottom of the castle, press Zoey's wings against the wall. It will make a beautiful painting to brighten up the White Room." She took a deep breath. "It's about time we decorated around here anyway."

My friends and I nodded at Mother Nature's instructions.

"Thank you," I said. "And we'll come back and see you soon."

With that, we stepped onto the table elevator and sunk down through the grass.

Back downstairs, Uncle T was waiting for us.

"You've had a busy morning," he said. "Time to rest."

He was definitely right.

"But first," Zoey said, "we have to do one thing." She walked to a wall and backed up to it, pressing her rose petal wings against the marble surface.

When she stepped away, a beautiful, bright rainbow appeared across the wall.

"Are my wings cleaned off?" she asked. She turned around so that we could see where the paint had been.

Zander and I nodded.

"All back to normal," I said.

And then it happened.

The light in the whole castle changed from white to a soft yellow.

"What's happening?" I asked, looking around. "What was that?"

Zoey and Zander also looked around. We were

all stunned.

Uncle T scanned the walls for a long moment. Then he smiled at us. "It's warmth," he said. "The castle likes having you here."

I looked at my friends and thought about what Uncle T said.

The castle likes having us here.

Maybe being there wasn't so bad, either. Not if we could find a cure for Mother Nature at least.

And I bet we could. With Zoey and Zander, I was pretty sure I could do anything.

I hugged each of them. "Thanks, you two," I said. "You're the best."

Then I took a deep breath and studied the rainbow on the wall.

It was time to start planning what to do next.

JEN CARTER

Sarafina and

the Muddy Mess

by Jen Carter

CHAPTER 1

THE BLUE KEY

Being Mother Nature probably sounds like a lot of fun. She gets to know all the plants and animals in the world, and helping them grow healthy and happy must seem interesting and exciting. But guess what? Being Mother Nature is also really tricky.

I've found that out the hard way. My twin sister, Aurelia, happens to be Mother Nature. But she got sick, and this morning, I had to take over for her.

What's tricky about it? For starters, there are four Elements that I also have to watch over: Air, Water, Earth, and Fire. I've only been on the job a couple hours, so I haven't met all of them yet. I can tell you this, though: *Air* is quite a rascal.

In fact, that's what he was doing right before my second adventure as Mother Nature began: being a rascal.

Whoosh! Whoosh! Whoosh!

"Air! What are you doing?" I laughed.

Whoosh! Whoosh! Whoosh!

I kept laughing as Air kept whooshing around me and my friends. We were right outside Mother Nature's castle, and Air was blowing strong gusts of winds at me and my friends, Zoey and Zander. First he'd blow in one direction until we almost fell over, and then right before we hit the ground, he'd blow in another direction. Once we almost hit the ground in that direction, he'd blow again from somewhere else.

Whoosh! Whoosh! Whoosh!

My curly, red hair was flying in my eyes, but I could still see my friends laughing nearby. Zander, my talking dog friend, was trying to run with the wind. He couldn't switch directions fast enough, though, so he looked like a flip-flopping fish out of water.

Whoosh! Whoosh! Whoosh!

Zoey, my fairy friend, stood still like me. When the wind caught in her pink rose petal wings, they became like the sails on a sailboat and dragged her across the grass. Her hair with the beautiful flowers growing out of it was all tangled her in face, just like mine. But just like me, she didn't seem to care.

Whoosh! Whoosh! Whoosh!

This was a fun game.

That is, until Air changed the game into something else. With each *whoosh*, he began to whisper something. At first, I barely heard it. I thought it was just the sound of the wind. But his whispers got louder with each gust.

I know something you don't know. I know something you don't know.

Whoosh! Whoosh! Whoosh!

I know something you don't know. I know something you don't know.

"What?" I yelled into the wind. "Air, what did you say?"

Whoosh! Whoosh! Whoosh!

I know something you don't know. I know something you don't know.

"Wait, wait!" Zander called. "Air, you know something? Tell us what you know, please!"

Air's voice got louder. "I'm not telling!" *Whoosh!*

Zoey had been blown a couple feet away from Zander and me, but the next gust of wind dragged her back over to us. "Pretty-please can you tell us?" she asked.

The wind stopped.

"Oh, don't you think it's more fun when I just tease you like this?" Air asked. *Whoosh!*

"No!" all three of us yelled at once.

Just then, a buzzing sound came from the belt on my yellow dress. I looked at it, and, sure enough, the key ring I had tied to it was vibrating. I touched each key until I came to the one that was buzzing like a swarm of unhappy bees.

It was the blue one.

"Oh boy," I said under my breath. And then to my friends, I explained, "It looks like we are needed back inside the castle."

"Which Element needs us?" Zoey asked as she leaned in to look at my belt.

"Not me!" Air said in a sing-song voice. "But I still know something you don't know!"

If Zander could have rolled his eyes at Air, I think he would have. But, being a dog, he couldn't—so he rolled his nose in a big circle.

"It's Water," I said. "We're being called back to the castle because something is going on with Water. C'mon, let's go."

We turned and hiked just a little ways up the hill to the front of the castle. When we came to the swirly, pinkish-white marble walls, I touched the smooth surface gently. I knew how to make a doorway appear for us to get into the castle, but I needed to take a deep breath first. The morning had been quite an adventure as I mixed-up a rainbow and then had to un-mix it up. I wondered what the next adventure was going to be. I hoped that I wasn't going to make any more mistakes along the way.

I looked at Zoey. "You have Mother Nature's purse?"

She nodded and patted the silvery purse hanging at her side. It looked like a regular purse, but it was filled with Aurelia's magical tools. My sister made the purse look ordinary so that if it ever got lost, no human would know it was magic. I had a feeling we were going to need it soon.

"Let's do this!" Zander said as he chased his tail in a circle.

"Here goes," I said under my breath. I pushed hard against the smooth castle wall, and a doorway appeared.

We walked through it.

Behind us, Air was still teasing us. "I know something you don't know, I know something you don't know!"

CHAPTER 2

SLIPPING AND SLIDING

The first room in the castle is called the White Room, and it's pretty bare. There's a black table with some chairs in the middle, and the walls are bright white. Before this morning, there wasn't anything at all decorating the walls—but now there was one decoration: a picture of the rainbow we fixed earlier.

My uncle was sitting at the table. The rest of the world knows him as Father Time, but since he's my uncle, I just call him Uncle T.

He looked exactly the same as ever. His blond hair was combed to the side. His shirt and tie looked clean and straight. He was scribbling on a piece of paper when we walked in. Without looking up, he said, "Back already?"

"The blue key is calling us, Boss," Zander said. He galloped over to Uncle T and sat at his feet. With his tongue hanging out the side of his mouth, Zander was practically begging Uncle T to pet him. But instead of petting my favorite dog in the world, Uncle T stood and looked at his watch.

"Let's see what's going on," he said. He began walking toward the back of the room.

Zander galloped over to me and Zoey. We scratched his head, and then all three of us followed Uncle T.

Three doors stood at the back of the White Room. Uncle T opened the middle door.

This time, walking into Isla's room wasn't as shocking as it was this morning. This time, I knew what to expect.

On a huge, silver throne sat Isla the peacock. Her name is pronounced *eye-la*. She helps us keep track of the Elements of Nature. If an Element like Air or Water is causing a problem, one of Isla's feathers lights up with a picture of what is happening. Then, once we know the problem, all we have to do is use the buzzing key in the door behind Isla. From there we are transported to wherever the problem is.

My sister came up with this system before she

got sick. It worked pretty well, even though I was still getting used to it.

"It's a good thing we already know Water," Zoey said as we walked to Isla.

I nodded. We *did* know Water. That morning, we had met her during the mixed-up rainbow adventure, but just barely. It wasn't a bad meeting, but it wasn't great. I'm not sure Water was impressed with my mixed-up rainbow.

We hadn't met Earth or Fire yet. I was glad that Fire wasn't calling us. I didn't really want to meet Fire. I bet she was really *hot*.

Isla sat on her silver throne looking like a queen. The feathers sticking out of her head reminded me of a crown. The fanned-out feathers behind her looked like a royal robe. As we neared her, we studied the white feather that was glowing. It showed a big lake surrounded by mountains. The lake was calm. No waves, no rain, no problems.

"Ah," Uncle T said. "Water wants to speak with you. You don't have to solve a problem right now. She just wants to meet."

I scrunched my eyebrows together. "How do you know?" I asked.

He nodded at the peacock feather. "Look. Nothing is going wrong in that picture. Also, that lake is Water's special place. That's her favorite spot in the world. When everything is peaceful, she hangs out there."

I looked at my friends. A relieved smile was on Zoey's face. I'm sure a relieved smile was also on my face, too. No problem to solve. That was good news.

"Let's go," Zander said. He pranced to the door that would take us to see Water.

Zoey and I skipped after him. I took the blue key off my belt and twisted it into the lock.

Last time I opened that door, it was with the yellow key. And it was to see Air. I wondered what would happen when we used the blue key to see Water.

I swung open the door and saw a shiny, white slide.

A slide this time?

"Huh," Zoey said. "No stairs?"

She was reading my mind. When we went to see Air, there was a staircase on the other side of the door. Not a slide. This was definitely different.

"Slides are awesome," Zander said. "Let's do this!"

The slide wasn't super-steep, but it twisted and turned in every direction for as far as I could see. There were tunnels and loops, back and forth, back and forth, more tunnels and more loops. I almost felt dizzy just looking at the curvy slide.

My stomach felt a little sick. This might be more scary than fun. But we didn't have a choice.

Zoey and I sat down next to each other and held hands. Zander jumped into our laps.

"Ready?" I asked with a deep breath.

Zander barked. Zoey nodded.

We pushed off. Suddenly, we were zooming away—much faster than I expected.

"*Weeeeeee!*" Zander laughed. His tongue wagged out the side of his mouth. A little slobber flew off and barely missed my cheek.

"*Whoaaaa!*" Zoey yelled.

"Hold on tight!" I said. I tried to squeeze my friends closer. The ride went on and on, twisting and turning, looping and tunneling. My hair was blowing all over my face. All I could see was a tangled red mess, and that
was probably a good thing. I was

scared enough already. I didn't need to see what was coming next and get more scared.

But then…

Zoey yelled words I didn't want to hear.

"*Ahhhh!* We're going to crash!"

"What do you mean?" I yelled back. Hair got

in my mouth making it hard to speak.

"Brace yourselves!" Zander yelled.

I pushed some red curls away from my eyes and saw what they meant. The slide was coming to an end. The lake was right in front of us. It looked like we would land on a big, green lily pad—but we were going so fast that we might fly right past the lily pad and land in the water. I clung to Zoey and Zander tighter, ducked my head, and closed my eyes.

"*Ahhh!*" all three of us yelled.

And then, right before we reached the lily pad, we slowed down, almost to a stop. For the last couple feet, we slowly inched to the lily pad and then plopped onto it.

I looked at my friends. My heart was pounding, and I was even a little out of breath. I wondered if they felt the same way. "That was a little scary," I said.

"That was amazing!" Zander said. He jumped off our laps and looked around. "Where are we?"

A gentle wave under us made the lily pad bobble just a little.

"Welcome," a voice said.

I remembered the voice from the mixed-up rainbow adventure that morning. It was Water's voice.

"Hi, Miss Water," I said. I looked all around. Where exactly was the voice coming from? The lake? The voice seemed to be all around us.

Zoey started to stand up. She was light on her feet and very graceful. Her wings fluttered just enough to help her stay balanced. "Hi Miss Water," she said.

"Hiya, Miss Water," Zander added.

I tried to stand up like Zoey and Zander. The lily pad was too wavy under my feet. "Whoa!" I said while making big arm circles to steady myself. The arm circles didn't work. I fell back on my rear end.

Zoey tried to help me up, but I shook my head. "I'll just sit," I whispered to her. Then to Water, I said louder, "How can we help you, Miss Water?"

"Sarafina," Water sniffed, "I have some questions for you."

Her words were slow and serious. They sent little ripples through the lake, and the lily pad vibrated.

Had I done something wrong? It sounded like I was in trouble.

"I heard that Aurelia is sick," Water said. "Why wasn't *I* told about this? I don't like to be left out when the safety of the world is at stake!"

I looked at Zoey and Zander. All our eyes grew.

Uh oh. I *was* in trouble.

CHAPTER 3

WORRIED WATER

I cleared my throat. "Well, Miss Water…"

I tried to think of something to say, but my mind was blank.

Finally, I said, "We just found out, too."

The lake rippled. So did the lily pad.

"Then how did *Air* find out before me? It's never a good idea for Air to know things. He's likely to cause more problems."

"Like the rainbow this morning?" Zander offered.

"Exactly," Water said.

Another wave rocked the lily pad.

"We can't keep him from causing trouble if he

knows so much," Water whined.

She brought up a good point, but I didn't know how to answer. If Air was listening, he was sure to be mad if I agreed with Water. But if I didn't agree with Water, she could get really upset. I didn't want her to send a big wave over the giant lily pad or make us sink.

I looked at my friends and lifted my palms to the sky. "What should I say?" I whispered.

Zoey cleared her throat. "We're sorry, Miss Water," she said while still fluttering her wings to stay balanced. Her eyes had turned green to match the lily pad. "If we hear any more big news, we'll tell you."

I gave Zoey a thumbs up and mouthed, "Good answer."

"Thank you," Water said with a sigh. "Now that we've agreed you promise to tell me *everything* before you tell Air *anything*, we have another important matter to discuss. How is Aurelia? Sarafina, how *is* your sister?"

I felt my face getting a little scrunched up. I didn't think we just promised Water what she said. But maybe now was not the time to argue. Maybe it was just better to answer her question about Aurelia.

"Um," I began, "well, she's sick."

"Oh, I know that!" Water said. "But what kind of sick? Does she have a cold? A tummy ache? Or is it something worse like Piggy-pox or Wilty-bark? Oh no, don't tell me she has Bandy-standy-foo!"

Zoey gasped. Zander let out a little yelp. I nearly yelped, too. What was Bandy-standy-foo? Just hearing the name gave me the shivers. It sounded like something that would involve purple polka-dots—or worse.

"Miss Water," I said slowly, "we don't know what Piggy-pox is. Or what Wilty-bark is. Or flandy-foo-what's it again?"

"If she had them, you would know," Water answered. "Good! I'm glad that we can rule those out. If you don't know what's wrong, you must go find out."

"We don't know how to find out," I said. "Aurelia doesn't know what's wrong. Neither does Uncle T."

"Then you haven't got a second to lose, my dears. You must go check on her at once to see if she's gotten worse. And then, of course, you must report back to me. Go, at once!"

Zander bounced in a circle and then crouched down with his tail in the air. He was ready to go.

He knew an order when he heard one. He just didn't quite know where to go.

Zoey touched my arm. "Sarafina, how do we get back to the castle?" she asked. "Slides only go one direction. Down."

"Do we walk back?" Zander asked. He neared the slide and pawed it.

"Just sit back down on the slide the way you were before," Water said.

Zoey lightly leaped over to the slide. Zander jumped onto her lap. I scrambled on my hands and knees over to them and took my place.

Suddenly, I felt something tugging me backward. It felt like a bar had been put across my stomach and was pulling me up the slide. I bet my friends felt the same thing.

"Here we go!" Zoey squealed. She squeezed my hand and hugged Zander's neck tighter.

Soon we were zooming upward and backward.

"Wheee!" Zander sang. He could look where we were going from his spot on our laps. Zoey and I could only see our hair in our eyes again.

I was feeling dizzy with all the zigging and zagging. It's one thing to go down a slide facing forward. It's totally different going backward. I squeezed my eyes tight and hung on tight.

Then, just when I thought I couldn't take it

any longer, the slide spit us back into Isla's room. We landed with a thud on the floor. Zander immediately jumped off our laps and sat next to us.

"I love that slide," he said.

Zoey and I didn't move. I think we were both too dizzy.

"Ow," I said while trying to shake the dizziness out of my head. "I don't think I love that slide."

Zoey closed her eyes. "Me neither."

Uncle T's polished black shoes suddenly appeared next to us. I looked up to see the rest of him.

"Is all well with Water?" he asked while checking his wristwatch.

Zander inched over to him and looked up with the "please pet me!" tongue wag, but Uncle T didn't seem to notice.

As Zoey and I got to our feet, I said, "She said we have to find out what's wrong with my sister."

Uncle T shook his head and then looked at his pocket watch. "That's all she wanted? That wasn't a good use of time. Of course we need to find out what's wrong. We already knew *that*."

"Could it be Piggy-pox or Wilty-bark?" Zander asked.

Uncle T made a face. "Piggy-pox? Did Water say that?" He shook his head again. "Oh, her imagination is as wild as Air's imagination. Mother Nature certainly is not a pig, so she can't have Piggy-pox. And the last time I checked, she wasn't a tree, so Wilty-bark is out of the question."

"What about Bandy-standy-foo?" Zander asked. He inched closer, begging even more for Uncle T to pet him.

Uncle T looked down at Zander. He almost smiled. "That isn't even a real thing. Water must have made that one up."

My belt buzzed. My hand immediately went to the key ring, and I found the key that was vibrating.

"It's orange," I said. "The Animal Kingdom is calling us."

"Awesome," Zander said. "I've been waiting for this. Finally!" He laughed his wonderful dolphin laugh.

The three of us hurried out of Isla's room calling goodbye to Uncle T over our shoulders. We grabbed the Animal Kingdom door and flung it open.

I hoped there wasn't a big problem that needed solving. Solving problems wasn't my specialty—not yet at least.

Just one way to find out, I thought to myself.

CHAPTER 4

FISH IN THE MUD

Inside the Animal Kingdom, my friends and I stood together. Zoey linked her arm with mine. Zander wiggled between us and sat down to wait.

In front of us, twelve enormous bubbles bounced slowly up and down across a green field. Inside each one was a scene from a different part of the world. Each showed a different climate: hot climates, cold climates, wet climates, dry climates. You name it—there was a bubble for it.

"What do we do?" I asked. I knew that Zander had already explained the Animal Kingdom to me, but this was the first time we were *going* somewhere in the Animal Kingdom. Last time, we just looked at the bubbles. My stomach did a flip. Then a flop. Then a flip-flop.

I was nervous.

"Don't worry, Feenie," Zander said. His tail wagged back and forth across the grass. "One will come to us. All we have to do is walk into it. It'll take us wherever we need to go."

Just as the last word left his mouth, a bubble showing swampy-looking water bounced slowly in our direction.

"There it is!" Zander exclaimed. "The wetlands. Let's go!"

He ran full speed at the bubble and leaped into it. Suddenly, he was gone.

Zoey and I looked at each other and gasped.

"Where did he go?" Zoey squeaked.

I gulped. "The wetlands, I guess."

"We better go after him," Zoey said.

With our arms still linked, we tiptoed toward the giant bubble. I held my breath.

Don't be so scared, I told myself. *You already rode up a backwards slide today. Walking through a bubble is nothing.*

But that didn't help. I was still scared.

Zoey and I were about two inches from the bubble. We stared at the scene it pictured. There was so much mud with lots of tall grass sticking out of it. And there was Zander running around the tall grass sticking out of the mud.

"There he is," Zoey said. "It worked."

"Look at him," I said. "He's already so muddy." I made a face. "Oh, I really don't like mud."

"It'll be okay," Zoey said. "Let's go."

Together, we reached our hands out. As soon as we touched the bubble, we were sucked in. I heard a loud slurping sound all around me. Or was it a sucking sound? I couldn't tell. But then there was a big *pop*! And no more silly sounds.

Except for the squishy mud I was standing in.

Oh, yuck! I thought.

Zoey fluttered her fairy wings. They couldn't take her far, and they weren't fast, but they were strong enough to keep her feet out of the mud.

I, on the other hand, had to stand in the mud.

If only I could have given myself some wings. Maybe I could have, but it was not the time to try. With my luck, I might have ended up with horsetails sprouting out of my back by mistake.

"Hey! Hey! Over here!"

It was Zander. He was calling us from across the swampy swamp.

"I found out what's going on!" he yelled. "And you'll never guess what happened!"

I started stepping carefully through the mud toward him. It squished under my feet making slimy, burpy, mud noises. Zoey's wings fluttered extra fast to keep her toes off the ground most of the time. Every so often, she touched down, just barely, so that she could bounce right back into the air.

"How did he already figure out what happened?" I asked. "Weren't we only a couple seconds behind him getting here?"

"There's never a dull moment with Zander," Zoey said.

She was right. There was never a dull moment with either of my friends.

Zander was standing right in the middle of some really tall grass—it was taller than him, in fact. His paws were brown and gloppy with mud. His face was all muddy, too. His nose, his whiskers, his muzzle…all were wet and brown.

"Why were you sticking your face in the mud, Zander?" I asked.

He ran around in a happy circle, kicking up some mud. It splattered on my dress. I gasped without meaning to. *Yuck!*

"Oops!" He laughed, sounding like a dolphin. "I didn't mean to get you dirty. Sorry, I'm just so excited!"

"Why?" Zoey asked. "What happened?"

Zander laughed again.

"Well, you know how right after the mixed-up rainbow adventure Mother Nature said I had talents? I know what she meant now. "I can *talk* to fish."

Zoey and I both must have looked confused. I sure *felt* confused.

"Fish? What do you mean? You can talk to fish?" I looked around. "Zander, we're in the mud. There aren't even fish here."

Zander ran in another excited circle. More mud splashed on me. This time, I just took a deep breath and smiled. I had a feeling that I needed to get used to the mud.

And then, before Zander could answer, all kinds of little heads poked up through the mud. They were brown and slimy-looking, and they had teeny-tiny black eyes. I could tell they weren't worms—they were fatter than worms. But I didn't know what they were.

"Eek!" Zoey gasped. She flew a little higher and reached for me. Since she was in the air, the only part of me she could grab was my head. One of her hands grabbed a handful of messy hair. The other covered half my eye and smushed my cheek. Zander's tongue wagged out the side of his muddy mouth. Then he said, "These are *mudfish*. And they have an important message for us."

CHAPTER 5

A MUDDY WARNING

I moved Zoey's hand off my eye and made a confused face. "What do you mean?" I asked. "How do you know?"

"I can talk to them," Zander said. He bowed his head down to the mud and made some popping sounds with his tongue. Or was it his teeth? I couldn't tell.

When he looked up, he added, "I guess I laugh like a dolphin because I must have some sea life in me. I understand fish language."

Zoey let go of my head. She floated down a little, but not enough to touch the ground with her toes. Her eyes had turned brown to match the mud. "Uh, Zander, I'm sorry, but don't fish live in *water*? Are you sure these are fish?"

"Shh!" Zander whispered loudly. "They don't like it when people say that." He leaned down again and made more popping sounds.

Zoey and I looked at each other with wide eyes. "Wow," we both mouthed at the same time.

When Zander lifted his head, he said, "Okay, okay, I'll explain." He shook real hard, and mud went flying in all directions. It splashed across me and Zoey. "Oops!" he said, laughing a little. "Sorry, I can't help it sometimes."

Zoey shuttered and squeezed her eyes shut. But then she opened them and smiled. "It's okay," she said nicely. "You're a dog. You were born to shake."

"So," Zander said. "Mud fish live in the mud. Well, sometimes in mud and sometimes in water. They don't have to be in water all the time, so they were the perfect messengers for us. The sea animals needed to tell us something, but they couldn't tell us from the water. They didn't want Miss Water to hear."

My mouth dropped open.

A message from sea animals? A message that Miss Water couldn't hear? That sounded serious.

Zander hunched down to the slimy fish again.

More and more were poking through the mud every second. We were surrounded by those brown heads with teeny-tiny black eyes. There must have been thousands of them.

Zander made more popping sounds at the fish, and then he looked up to us.

"Well," he said slowly, "Miss Water is getting really upset about Mother Nature being sick. The more she thinks about it, the more upset she gets. She's starting to cause storms all over the place—even places where there aren't supposed to be storms."

Zoey fluttered down and let her toes touch the ground. "And the mudfish heard about this and wanted to warn us?"

Zander nodded. "Yes. Their cousins from the sea told them, and they told us. If animals in the water told us themselves, Miss Water would hear. And then she'd just get more upset that she was being tattled on."

"So what do we do?" I asked.

Zander turned his head back to the mud as though listening to the mudfish. After a moment, he looked up again. "Start thinking of ways to calm Water down."

Zander popped a couple more times, and then all the mudfish disappeared back into the swamp.

"They had to go," Zander said. "They have to get ready in case Miss Water comes along and starts storming over here, too."

I tried to think fast. "We better get back to the castle. We need to plan." I looked around the swamp. "Hey, how do we get back?"

"We just need to jump really hard," Zander said. "Jump like you want to pop the bubble. That will take us back."

"Jump on the *ground?* In the middle of this *swamp?*" Zoey asked. "What if that doesn't work? Then we'll be extra muddy!"

Zander laughed. "It's just a little mud. Nothing to worry about. Plus, if what the mudfish said is true, I think we'll be spending some time in a storm pretty soon. That will wash it all away."

Zoey nodded and sighed. She stopped fluttering her wings and let her feet sink all the way into the mud. She scrunched her face. "Yuck!" she moaned.

"On the count of three," I said. "One, two, three!"

Zoey and I jumped straight up. Zander jumped the only way he could—he leaped forward like he was going to pounce on a toy.

Suddenly we were back at the castle. We were in the Animal Kingdom room. Huge bubbles surrounded us, just like they had before our trip to the wetlands. The only thing that was different was our muddiness.

Oh, there was another difference: now we knew that Zander could talk to fish.

And we knew Water was throwing temper tantrums.

So I guess plenty had changed. The Animal Kingdom was the same, but we were different.
We started walking back to the White Room. We left a trail of mud behind us.

CHAPTER 6

TRICKY TOOLS

Uncle T was sitting at the black table when we walked through the door. He was shuffling some papers. When he looked up and saw the mud, he did not smile.

"Should I ask how you got so dirty?" he wondered aloud.

I shook my head. Zoey shook her head. Zander wagged his tail.

Then a question came to me, and I couldn't stop myself from asking.

"Does my sister ever come back covered in mud or drenched by rain?"

Uncle T glanced at the ceiling where my sister's

room was hidden. "No," he said. "But every Mother Nature is different. Not good, not bad, just different."

"Mud is fun," Zander said.

Zoey giggled. "Mud is muddy."

Uncle T made a *tsk tsk* sound and shook his head. Then he motioned for us to sit down at the table. "What is going on in the Animal Kingdom?" he asked.

Zander jumped on a chair and said, "The mudfish told us that Water is upset about Mother Nature being sick. They warned us that she's starting storms all over the place. Even where storms shouldn't be."

Uncle T tapped his fingers on the table and thought hard. Then he looked at his wristwatch.

"What's your plan?" he asked.

My eyes grew. Plan? I needed a plan?

"I don't have a plan, Uncle T," I said slowly. "But I bet we'll come up with something soon." I looked at my friends. Then I looked back at Uncle T. In a softer voice, I added, "Uh, do you have any suggestions?"

Uncle T shuffled more of his papers. "Think about what's in Mother Nature's purse." He nodded toward Zoey, who had the purse strapped across her chest. "See if anything in there might be useful." He stood up. "I have an appointment. I'll see you all soon, I'm sure."

He walked quickly across the room and went into the Plant Kingdom.

"Bye!" I called after him.

I don't think he heard because he didn't answer.

Zoey took off Mother Nature's purse and held it up. "Let's look through here."

"Hey!" Zander said. "Maybe we can go see Mother Nature. She can tell us how all the tools work."

Zoey and I both nodded our heads, agreeing to Zander's great idea.

I looked at the ceiling where my sister's room was. It was invisible to people who were not invited to see it. In fact, it just looked like a big skylight before we were invited to see it.

Uncle T thought I would be able to rise to Aurelia's room by using my mind one day. Today was not that day, though. I still had a lot to learn. For now, we would go up the old fashioned away.

I tapped the black table. "Down," I commanded. The table sunk into the floor. We stepped on it. "Up," I said. The table began rising like an elevator to the top of the castle.

My sister's room looks just like my special

garden down the hill. And just like last time we visited her, this time we had to go through the dirt and grass that made up Aurelia's bedroom floor. Everything looked brown for a second. Then it looked green. It smelled like earth. Then everything looked like sky and the garden. We were there.

Aurelia was in the same place as last time. She was resting against a tree, but this time she had a blanket of flowers pulled across her lap. And this time she was asleep.

"Should we wake her?" I whispered to my friends.

Zoey and Zander looked at each other and then shook their heads.

"I don't think that's a good idea," Zoey said.

"She needs her sleep," Zander added.

I studied my sister. My friends were right—Aurelia needed her sleep. I always thought of my sister smiling, and when she smiled, her cheeks were big and happy. Now, her cheeks were so flat and small they almost looked like they had disappeared. The purple circles around her eyes looked darker.

Is she getting worse? I wondered.

I decided not to think about it. Uncle T was right. I just needed a plan.

JEN CARTER

Then it came to me. Before I could stop the words from coming out of my mouth, I told my friends about it.

"I know," I said while pacing back and forth across the grassy floor. I used my fingers to count off the steps of the plan. "First, figure out how to use Mother Nature's tools in the purse. Second, figure out how to keep Water from causing big storms. Third, figure out how to cure Mother Nature."

I stopped pacing and looked at my friends. They looked back with big eyes and their mouths hanging open.

"What do you think?" I asked.

Slowly they both nodded.

"It's a good plan," Zoey said.

"It's just a lot to do," Zander said.

"And *how* do we do those things?" Zoey added.

They were both right. We had our goals. But how could we reach those goals? I had no idea.

Zoey sat down on the grass. "Let's look at the stuff in the purse while we're here. If Mother Nature wakes up, then we can ask her questions." Zoey reached inside the purse and unpacked it. "Here's some money, a phone, some makeup, a mirror, a hairbrush…"

"I wonder what they do," Zander said. "The brown makeup turned into rainbow paint. The other things must do amazing things, too."

I wished my sister would wake up so I could ask.

"Let's see," Zoey said. She picked up the hairbrush. It had a pink handle and black bristles. She examined the handle closely. Then she squeezed it. Suddenly all the bristles shot out of the brush. They looked like long, skinny, black threads flying across the garden.

"Eeek!" Zoey squealed. Then she laughed. "I didn't expect that."

I looked at the long, skinny threads that lay across the grass. "Me neither!"

Zander galloped over to the threads and sniffed the hairbrush bristles. "We better learn to expect anything," he said. "Do you think it's meant to reach out and catch stuff? Or maybe it's supposed to shoot stuff out—like a bunch of seeds that need to be planted."

I shook my head. "I have no idea."

Zoey twisted the hairbrush handle, and suddenly the bristles shrunk back into it. "Crazy," she said.

I looked at the other items from the purse that were laying on the ground. I was a bit scared to pick up anything after the hairbrush, but I knew I had to.

I reached for a blue pen. It had a button at one end. I pushed it, and suddenly the other end started making a swooshing sound.

Zander galloped back to us. He and Zoey leaned forward to listen more.

"I think..." I said slowly. "I think it's sucking..." Carefully, I put my finger to the end that was making the noises.

I was right. The pen sucked my finger to it. It was strong, too. I waved my hand over my head with the pen attached to my finger. It didn't come off.

"It's a vacuum," Zoey said.

"Good to know," Zander said.

I nodded. I clicked the top of the pen, and suddenly the vacuum stopped.

That wasn't so bad. Definitely not as scary as the shooting hairbrush. I was a little less scared about trying out another thing from the purse.

I reached for the coins. Before I could touch them, the keys on my belt vibrated.

"Uh-oh," I said. Before I even looked at the belt, I guessed which one was probably vibrating.

It had to be the blue one. The one for Water.

I looked down. Yep. It was blue. Water.

"If the mudfish were right, it's time to see what kinds of storms Water has started," I said.

"We can finish this later," Zoey said.

We stared packing up Mother Nature's purse. Once everything was back in, Zoey put the purse over her head and her shoulder to keep it safely in place.

"Let's hop to it," Zander said. "Maybe there will be some fish for me to talk to."

"We'll find out soon," Zoey said. She smiled, and her green eyes almost sparkled.

We stood on the magic table-elevator.

"Down!" I commanded.

As we sunk through the floor, I waved at my sleeping sister.

CHAPTER 7

WEEPY WATER

The White Room was empty when we got back. Uncle T must have been in the Plant Kingdom still. We dashed to Isla's room.

Inside the room, one of Isla's feathers was it up. We looked at the glowing circle and saw a terrible rainstorm. It looked like the land was bare—no grass, trees, or flowers. It was just dirt for miles and miles. Dirt and *lots* of rain water splattering everywhere.

"It's good that no one is there," I said. "The storm can't hurt anyone."

Zoey groaned. "But look." She pointed at the feather. "That's not a place where there is normally a lot of rain. It's just dirt. Plants don't really grow there. Do you know what that means?"

I shook my head. Zander's ears perked up.

"It means," Zoey said, "that the ground is going to have a hard time soaking up all the water. It's not used to getting so much rain. And that means…"

I knew what she was going to say.

Together, my friend and I said, "Flood!"

"Exactly," Zoey said. "And there might not be people right there, but who knows where the flood could end up going?"

"We've got to go talk to Water," I said.

Zander was already running to the door. Zoey and I followed. I used the blue key to open it.

We saw the same slide as before and hopped on.

Here we go, I thought. I closed my eyes and held my breath.

Just like last time, we zigged and zagged down the slide at full speed. This time I held my hair down to keep it from flying all over, but I kept my eyes shut. I knew we were almost at the end when Zander stopped saying *wha-hoo!*

The slide plopped us down on a lily pad again, but the lily pad wasn't floating on a lake like before. It was sitting in a big field of sloppy, squishy, slippery mud.

But we weren't getting wet, which reminded me of the mixed-up rainbow adventure that morning. There must have been an invisible dome around us keeping the rain and mud out.

Rain beat against the invisible barrier. It was so loud—it almost sounded like thunder.

"Miss Water!" I yelled to the sky. I could barely hear my own voice. "Are you okay?"

Rain hit the dome harder. I wanted to cover my ears.

"Oh, Sarafina!" Water wailed. "Is that you? I can barely see you through all my tears. *Whaaaaaa!*"

My friends and I looked at each other. Was Water *crying*? Was this storm caused by her crying?

"I didn't know that Water actually cried," Zander said.

Zoey sort of nodded and shook her head at the same time, like she was really confused. Her eyes were light brown to match the mud all around us. "I didn't either," she said. "How does Water cry?"

My head was starting to hurt. This was too strange. I wondered if the raindrops were salty like tears.

Oh Sarafina, stop letting your imagination get the best of you! I reminded myself. Of course rain wasn't salty.

"*Whaaaaa!*" Water continued to sob.

"Miss Water," I yelled, "we are worried about you. What's wrong?"

"*Whaaaa!* Sarafina, I can't hear you. You have to speak—*whaaaaaa*—you have to speak up!"

"I don't think you have to speak up," Zander grumbled, laying down and covering his ears with his paws. "She just has to calm down. You're loud enough already."

Zander was right. But I wasn't going to say *that*.

"Miss Water?" I yelled. "If you stop crying, maybe I can take down this dome and we can talk about what is bothering you. What do you say? Maybe we can help you."

Water sniffed. The rain got lighter. And then a little lighter. Then it looked like it was gone.

"Okay," Water said. She sniffed and took a deep breath. "I think I can talk now."

I closed my eyes and concentrated really hard on taking the barrier down. *Disappear, disappear, disappear*, I said silently. *Please disappear.*

After a few moments, the air got colder. I opened my eyes. A light mist was landing on us, and I knew the dome was gone.

"What's wrong, Miss Water?" I asked. Finally I

didn't have to yell. "We don't want you to be sad."

The mist started to get a little thicker. Then, with a wobbly voice, Water said, "I'm just so sad about your sister. I don't want her to be sick!" She paused a moment. And then suddenly she started crying again. "*Whaaaa!*"

Mud splattered onto the lily pad. Rain drops—or, I mean, tear drops—began drenching our hair.

"Quick, can you put the dome back up?" Zoey asked.

I shook my head hard, trying to keep water out of my eyes. "I don't know. If I do, she won't be able to hear us. I think we'll have to fix this in the rain."

"We better be fast," Zander said. "Look at the ground. There's so much rain that it's forming big puddles everywhere."

Zoey squeezed my arm. "Before we know it, all those puddles will join together and form a big—"

"—Flood!" we all said together.

CHAPTER 8

CHEERING UP WATER

"We have to cheer her up," Zoey said.

I nodded. Zoey was right. But how could we cheer up Water?

I needed time to think. There was never enough time to think!

Suddenly, I heard a different voice all around us. It wasn't Water...and it wasn't Air. Who was it?"

"Ugh!" it said. "What is this slop?"

My friends and I turned around and around. We couldn't figure out where the voice was coming from.

"Oh, oh, oh!" Water sobbed. "Earth, leave me

alone. I'm in no mood for your complaining!"

Something rumbled all around us. The ground might have even shaken a little.

"If *you* leave me alone, *I* will leave you alone!" Earth said. "This land isn't meant to be so wet. Go cry somewhere else."

I put both hands on my head. This was getting worse by the second. First, Water was almost causing a flood. Second, Earth was mad at her. And we hadn't even met Earth yet. How were we going to calm *her* down when we didn't even know her?

Zoey started digging in Mother Nature's purse.

"There has to be something in here to help us," she said.

"Good idea," Zander said.

I pushed wet hair off my forehead and leaned toward Zoey so I could see the purse better.

"How about the magic paint we used for the rainbow?" I asked.

"Feenie!" Zander said. "I have an idea." He jumped toward me, and I grabbed his front paws so that he was standing on two feet like a human. In my ear, he whispered, "You talk to Water and Earth. Just keep them distracted so that they don't start fighting or make things worse. Zoey and I will figure out if any of Mother Nature's tools will help at the same time."

Oh, that Zander. He's always full of ideas.

I nodded and let go of his paws. He scrambled over to Zoey. His nails made funny scraping noises on the lily pad as he barely kept his balance, but he didn't seem to care. He and Zoey started whispering.

"Miss Water? Miss Earth?" I called loudly. "Everything is going to be fine, I promise." I tried to sound really happy, and I smiled as big as I could.

"But, how do you know-*ow-ow-ow*?" Water sobbed. The puddles around me were getting bigger.

"I just saw my sister before we came here," I said.

Water gasped. The rain stopped again. "You did? Really?"

I nodded. "And she was doing okay," I said. "She was napping in her room." I raised my palms to the sky and gave a little shrug. "She just needs rest. Being Mother Nature is a big job. I think she just needs a break."

The ground vibrated a little.

"No other Mother Nature ever needed a break," Earth grumbled.

Water let out another small sob. "That is *true-ue-ue!*"

I had to think quickly. I didn't want Water starting to cry again.

I looked over at Zoey and Zander. They had the hairbrush out. Zoey pushed the handle and all the bristles flew out. Nothing happened. Nothing except the bristles landing in the mud next to the lily pad and getting all yucky.

Zoey shrugged at Zander and stared cranking the handle to get the bristles back in the brush.

Yikes, I thought. *That's not going well.*

"You're right," I said to Water and Earth. "But Mother Nature never had a sister either. There's a first for everything."

Earth grumbled an unhappy, huffy laugh. "Huh. That's true. Like this land getting so muddy. That's a first, too."

"Don't tease me, Earth," Water wailed. "I'm sa-*a-a-ad!*"

"It's okay to be sad," Earth said. "But be sad without crying all the time. I don't like being turned into a sloppy mess."

I squeezed my eyes shut and put my fingers in my ears as they started bickering. Big drops of rain began falling. The water on the ground was now an inch thick. It had covered the lily pad and was over my toes.

The last time I used my Mother Nature talents, I mixed up a rainbow. I didn't want to try using my talents again and make another mistake. I couldn't think of anything else to do, though. Water and Earth weren't going to listen to me any other way.

Keeping my eyes and ears shut, I concentrated as hard as I could.

Stop raining. Send this water away. Send it back. Go away, rain! Go back to where you came from!

Suddenly, I felt something cold flicking the bottom of my nose. And then under my chin. And then the bottom of my lip. And then whatever it was, it flew up my nose.

I opened my eyes and unplugged my ears. Water and Earth were still bickering. Water might have still been raining, but I couldn't tell—because now little droplets of muddy water were flying upward to the sky.

Oh no.

Go back, I had said. *Go back to where you came from*. The rain, now brown and dirty from already landing in the mud, was going back to where it had come from. And some of it was flying up my nose in the process. The drops seemed confused, too. They didn't go straight up. They were zig zagging all around. Maybe that was because they were fighting against gravity.

I tried to wipe the dirty water off my face. Zoey and Zander were still trying out Mother Nature's tools, but now they were trying to keep muddy water droplets off of themselves, too. We were getting covered in brown polka dots as the water flew in the wrong direction and landed on our skin, clothes, and fur.

That's not what I wanted to happen.

I had to try something.

"Water! Earth!" As I yelled out the Elements' names, zig-zagging droplets flew into my mouth. They tasted, well, *dirty*. I spat out the yucky water. Then I covered my mouth and tried again. "Water! Earth!" My words were muffled, but at least I wasn't getting confused water drops in my mouth. "I'm worried about my sister too, but instead of getting sad, let's see how we can help her. Let's see if we can fix the problem."

Water sniffed. She didn't seem to notice the water droplets flying up to the sky.

"Hey, now you're talking," Earth said. "Let's not focus on how bad the problem is. Let's focus on how to solve the problem before it gets worse."

From the corner of my eye I looked at Zoey

and Zander. Zoey had just thrown some silver coins into the air. They splattered in the mud when they landed. Zander ran after them and brought them back. He shook water out of his fur, and Zoey didn't even flinch when it got all over her.

I bit my lip. I guess throwing coins didn't make them do anything special. And I guess Zoey was getting used to being spotted with muddy water.

"Hey, Water?" Earth said. "I bet we could get this figured out. If we just work together, we could find a way to cure Mother Nature."

"Exactly!" I exclaimed. "We can definitely solve this."

"You're right, Earth," said Water. She seemed like she was ignoring my last words. "We just have to think."

"Let's call a meeting," Earth said. "Let's head back to our favorite spots and start holding meetings with the plants and animals. We'll get the animals to put their heads together. And since the plants don't have heads, they'll put their leaves together. We can come up with something."

"Great idea," Water said.

And then, suddenly, they were gone. Water and Earth were gone. Those two Elements just left us there without so much as a goodbye.

I looked at Zoey and Zander. With my hands still over my mouth, I asked, "Problem solved?"

Zoey faked a smile at me. Zander lay on the lily pad and covered his eyes with his paws. He was half under water.

"Sort of solved," Zander said, lifting his head. "Water and Earth are gone and they stopped fighting." He dropped his nose back under the water like he wanted to hide.

"But look at this place," Zoey said. "We are ankle deep in water and mud." She batted down some dirty, zig-zagging water droplets away from her face. "And weird water is flying around everywhere."

Just then, another voice was all around us. A familiar voice.

"Hey there, kiddos," it said.

Air! It was Air!

"Hey Air," I said. "How are you?"

"I heard there was a meeting about curing Mother Nature. I came as fast as I could. We can start the meeting now that I'm here!"

Zoey and Zander looked at me with worried faces. I looked back at them with the same worried face.

"Yes, I think you're right," I said slowly. "Water and Earth just left to have a meeting about

Mother Nature. I don't know where they went though. Their favorite places, maybe?"

A gust of strong wind blew at us. My tangled, wet hair slapped against my face, and I almost fell over. Zoey grabbed Mother Nature's purse and held it tight to make sure it didn't fly away.

"What?" Air bellowed. "They left without me?"

Oh no, I thought. He was mad. *Problem NOT solved.*

CHAPTER 9

OH, AIR

"They are always leaving me out," Air whined.

Another gust of wind blew hard at us. I should have been ready for it, but I wasn't. I fell backward and splashed muddy water everywhere.

I was already pretty wet, but now my clothes were soaking in cold, brown water. At least I was on the lily pad, which meant that I wasn't sitting on squishy mud. I was just surrounded by muddy water.

I didn't get up. If I got up, Air was probably just going to knock me down again. Better to stay down.

"This isn't fair," Air continued. "I'm supposed

to be the one who knows things that you don't know. I knew that Water was starting to throw fits and storms everywhere before you did. How come I didn't know about the meeting before you?"

I remembered back to the silly game Air had been playing with us before the mudfish called. *I know something you don't know*, he kept saying.

I didn't mind him knowing things that I didn't know. If it made him happy, and if it made him want to play fun games, that was fine with me. That was *way* better than him being mad and knocking us into dirty water.

"Air, I'm sure they didn't mean to," I said. "I don't think they knew you were coming."

"But I'm always coming," Air said. "I'm *Air*. I'm always moving. I'm always going somewhere. They should have known that!"

Zoey stood with her feet wide apart, firmly planted on the lily pad. Her wings were too wet to fly, and she looked worried that Air was going to push her over into the disgusting water.

Zander was still lying down. He looked up. "It was much easier talking to mudfish," he muttered under his breath.

He took a deep breath, and then he covered his face with his paws again.

"Earth and Water probably really need your

help," I said to Air. "They were arguing before they called the meeting. Maybe you could help them be nice." Rain flying in the wrong direction stung my cheeks and the corners of my eyes. I tried to blink it away since my hands were too wet to wipe it away.

"Hmph!" Air said. "If I had arms, I would cross them. And if I had feet, I would stamp them. But I don't. So I will just blow!"

And, with that, the biggest gust of wind came at us. It was so strong that all three of us slid right off the lily pad and into the mud.

Splat! Glop! Shmash! Blurp! The disgusting mud made every horrible sound possible as we fell into it.

Zoey looked like a drooping, brown flower with her sad, soaked wings. Zander looked like a giant mudfish. I probably looked like a chocolate popsicle.

Air sighed. He blew a slight breeze by. "Ah, I feel much better now. I just had to get that out of my system, I guess. You're right. They will need my help. I'll go find them."

And then Air was gone.

I tried to wipe mud away from my eyes, but I think I just smushed it around my face even more. And then I tried standing up, but I fell back to the ground and splashed my friends.

"Was that really necessary?" Zoey asked. She tried to stand up, too, but she slipped and landed back in the mud with one leg on Zander and one wing on me. "Did he really need to blow us into the mud?"

I shook my head and helped Zoey sit up straight. It was probably better if we didn't try to stand.

"No, that wasn't necessary," I said. "But I think that's just how Air is sometimes."

Together, Zoey and Zander shook their heads and mumbled, "Oh, Air."

And then in a flash, he was back.

"Oh," Air said quickly. "I forgot. To clean up this mess, use Mother Nature's pen. Gotta go. Smooches!" He made a *mwah* sound like he was blowing a kiss, and then he left again.

My friends and I looked at each other with surprised faces.

The pen—what a great idea!

Maybe it could suck up all this mud.

"Oh, Air!" we all said. This time, we said it happily.

Zoey pulled the pen from Mother Nature's purse. Luckily, mud hadn't gotten inside it. She handed the pen to me.

"Okay, here we go," I said softly. I pointed the writing end toward the yucky, brown water and then pressed the cap. A loud vacuuming sound filled the air. A moment later, the pen began sucking up the water all around us.

"It's working!" Zander said.

I could tell he wanted to run in a circle because he was so excited. But he didn't—not yet. He was waiting until all the muddy water was gone.

Slurp, suck, slurp, suck! The pen kept vacuuming away.

"I wonder how much it can hold," I said.

"Probably as much as it needs," Zoey said. "Hopefully."

She seemed to be right. The pen kept sucking. Far, far off in the distance, I could see the land getting drier. The water was all disappearing into the pen, and soon the wet area was getting smaller and smaller...until all the water was completely gone. And the best part was that there wasn't any more dirty rain left to zig-zag up to the sky.

I turned off the pen. It stopped vacuuming.

"It's not any heavier than it was before," I said with a laugh.

I handed it back to Zoey. She put it in the purse.

"Well, that was interesting," Zander said. He

walked away from us and shook out his fur. He looked like a porcupine suddenly. "Shall we head back to the castle?"

Zoey and I looked at each other and nodded. Then I smiled. We might have been muddy, but the flood had been taken care of.

We trudged over to the slide and zoomed back up to the castle.

CHAPTER 10

CONCENTRATING ON CLEAN

When we got back to the castle, Uncle T was standing in Isla's room. He took one look at us and his eyebrows rose.

"Good trip?" he asked.

"Good enough," Zander said. He pranced over to Uncle T and looked up with his *please pet me* eyes.

Uncle T nodded. Then he turned and walked toward the White Room without petting Zander.

I couldn't be sure, but I think Isla might have stared at us with surprised eyes as we left her room. I bet Mother Nature never came back looking the way we did.

Back at the black table, Uncle T sat down. We sat down, too, but it wasn't pleasant. Our wet, muddy clothes (and fur) made wet, squishy sounds. I felt slippery and cold.

"Anything new?" Uncle T asked.

I looked at my friends. Then I said, "Earth and Water have decided to call a meeting with plants and animals. They want to put their heads and leaves together and find a cure for Mother Nature. I think Air might be helping, too."

Uncle T's eyebrows rose again. "Put their heads and leaves together?"

I shrugged. "That's what they said."

Uncle T sighed and then looked at his watch. "You all need to get cleaned up. If those three elements are planning something, you need to be prepared for whatever might come next. And if Fire gets involved, watch out. The four of them together will cause more problems than they solve."

"I'm not surprised," Zander said. He laughed like a dolphin.

Zoey and I laughed, too. After the muddy mess, laughing felt good.

"So, where do we go to get cleaned up?" I asked.

Uncle T thought a moment. "You might be

able to do it with your mind. Just concentrate hard on new, clean clothes. That's what Mother Nature would do."

I had a feeling that wasn't going to work. A mixed-up rainbow and flying rain way proved I wasn't good at concentrating just yet.

"If I can't do that, what should I do?" I asked.

Uncle T glanced at the ceiling. "We can go see if your sister is awake and ask her what she thinks." He looked at the clock on the end of his tie. Then he stood. "I have a meeting in the Animal Kingdom. I'll be back soon." He headed toward the Animal Kingdom door and disappeared through it.

I looked at my friends.

"Go ahead and try, Feenie," Zander said. "I'm sure you can get us cleaned up, easy-peasey."

Zoey reached across the table and touched my arm. "Wait—before you do, let's make sure we can remember this adventure." She pointed to the rainbow on the wall. "We'll never forget the mixed-up rainbow because we have that great picture there. We need a reminder of this adventure, too."

I smiled at my friends. Zander's tongue hung out the side of his mouth happily. Zoey's eyes matched the blue in the rainbow picture perfectly.

We walked to the wall next to the rainbow. Zoey and I pressed our muddy hands to the marble surface. Zander jumped onto his hind legs and pressed his front paws next to our handprints.

The light in the castle changed, just like it did when we put the rainbow picture on the wall. It went from a soft yellow to a slightly brighter yellow.

We all smiled.

The castle likes having us here, I thought. That's what Uncle T had said. He must have been right. It kept brightening.

I felt better. I was still worried about my sister, but it was nice to know that the castle liked having us there.

"Okay," I said. I rubbed my hands together. "Ready to see if I can clean us up by myself?"

"Yes!" Zoey and Zander sang out.

I closed my eyes and concentrated on clean clothes. *A clean yellow dress for me. A clean pink dress for Zoey. Clean Golden Retriever fur for Zander. Untangled hair for me. Dry flower hair for Zoey.*

Concentrate, concentrate, concentrate! I told myself.

I opened my eyes. My dress was clean, but it was green with little white polka dots on it. And it was on backward. The zipper went all the way up to my chin, and the bow covered almost all of my stomach.

Zoey's dress was clean, too, but it was purple with yellow squiggly lines. Also, it was inside out. Luckily, Mother Nature's purse was still over her shoulder—and it still looked exactly the same. Her hair was dry, but the flowers in it had grown bigger.

Zander's fur was clean, but it was standing up everywhere. He looked like a puffball.

"Wow!" Zoey and Zander said. They were looking at me with wide eyes.

"What?" I asked. I felt my hair. It was dry, but there was something different about it.

"Your hair looks like a big tower! It's sticking straight up!" Zoey said.

"I love it," Zander said.

I giggled. My hair did feel like a tower. I couldn't even touch the top.

"Well, we're clean," I said. "But I still need to work on this concentration thing."

"We look great," Zander said. He ran around in a circle, chasing his tail.

I giggled again. He had no idea that he looked like a puffball, but I was sure his fur would settle back into place.

"Let's go see if Aurelia is awake," I said. "I'd

like to say hello."

Zoey and Zander nodded.

I tapped the black table and it sunk to the ground. We stepped on and began moving upward toward the ceiling.

As we rose, I wondered how the meeting with Water, Earth, and Air was going.

Maybe Uncle T was right. Maybe they were going to cause more problems than they solved. But maybe he was wrong. Maybe they could fix Mother Nature.

Maybe they already had.

Soon, we would find out. I was sure of it.

Sarafina and

the Bouncy Island

by Jen Carter

CHAPTER 1

NOT LOVEY DOVEY

I always knew that being Mother Nature wasn't easy. There's a lot to do when taking care of plants and animals—even *I* knew that. But it wasn't until I had to take over my sister's job as Mother Nature that I found out just how hard it was.

I'm trying my best, but I still make mistakes. Like this morning, I mixed up the colors of a rainbow. Then this afternoon, I almost let a flood happen in the middle of a desert. Luckily, my friends and I managed to stop it, but not before getting covered in mud.

And on top of doing Mother Nature's job, I've realized that I *have* to find a cure for whatever is making my sister sick. She has to get better, and not just because I don't want to keep making mistakes while doing her job. Because she's my sister, and I care about her. I want her to be well.

That's exactly what I was thinking about as my third adventure doing Mother Nature's job.

How can we cure Aurelia?

"Here we go," I said to my two friends who were helping me. I glanced at both of them as the platform elevator took us closer and closer to Aurelia's hidden room in the castle. Zoey, my fairy friend had closed her eyes as we rose toward the ceiling. Zander, my trusty Golden Retriever friend, was wagging his tail and letting his tongue hang out the side of his mouth.

Then, before I could close my eyes like Zoey, everything smelled like dirt and grass. And everything was brown and green.

I should have been used to it. I'd visited my sister's room before, and this happened every time. Still, the smells and colors were so strong and bright that it surprised me.

Once we finished rising through the ceiling—and through the ground of my sister's enchanted garden bedroom—the smell of dirt and grass drifted away. I was glad to be through the dirt and even gladder that I spotted my sister quickly.

"There she is," I whispered to my two friends. I pointed at Aurelia resting against a tree. She had a blanket of flowers pulled over her lap, and she looked peaceful as she slept.

It was almost like looking in a mirror. She and I both had red, curly hair. We both had some freckles on our cheeks. There were only two differences between us. First, I had stayed looking like a child when she was picked to become the next Mother Nature all those years ago, but she grew into an adult. That was the biggest difference. The other difference was that she was definitely sick. The skin under her eyes was almost purple, and her cheeks were more pale than normal.

"She's still sleeping," Zoey said.

I glanced at my friend. The flowers in her hair moved gently in the breeze, and her eyes changed to match the color of the grass. Zoey was *very* in-tune with the plants around her.

I nodded. Aurelia had also been asleep the last time we visited her. We didn't wake her then, and I thought we probably shouldn't wake her this time either.

I *did* want to wake her, though. We needed to talk to her about coming up with a cure for her sickness.

"We better let her sleep," Zander said.

I looked at my other best friend. Yep, talking was one of his special talents. Not only that, but also when he laughed, he sounded like a dolphin. All of that was pretty amazing, but it got even better: just that afternoon, we found out he could talk to sea life.

"You're right," I said. I felt my heart sinking just a bit. Even though he was right about letting Aurelia sleep, I was still disappointed.

I looked around the garden. It was just like my home down the hill from the castle. There were beautiful trees everywhere, a nice ocean breeze, and butterflies flying around. It made me miss my own garden.

I know that might seem strange since Aurelia's room looked *exactly like* my home. But it still wasn't my home. It was my sister's enchanted room in the castle.

Just then, Zander said, "Look!"

He stared off in the distance. His back went stiff. His ears perked up. He was ready to run after something.

Zoey and I looked in the same direction, but we didn't see anything.

"What is it?" Zoey asked.

"Doves," Zander said. "There are two white doves in that tree over there. We don't ever see doves in this garden. What are they doing here?"

Good question, I thought. If Mother Nature's

room was really like our garden, it wouldn't have something in it that didn't belong in our garden. Would it?

An idea came to me.

"Zander, want to go ask them what they're doing?" I asked. "We just found out you can talk to fish. Maybe you can talk to birds, too."

"Yes!" Zander trotted toward the tree with the birds. Zoey fluttered her wings just a little and began skipping after Zander. I tried to keep up, but I'm not a dog with four legs or a fairy with wings. I don't move as fast.

"*Cooooo!*" Zander said, sounding just like a bird. "*Cooooooo!*"

I smiled. Maybe Zander really could talk to all different kinds of animals. *What an amazing talent*, I thought.

As soon as we got to the tree, the two birds flew away.

"*Coooo! Cooo, cooo, coooo!*" Zander called after them.

But they just kept flying, higher and higher, farther and father into the sky. They cooed and cooed back to Zander, but the further they flew, the harder it was for us to hear them.

"What did you say to them, Zander?" Zoey asked.

"I just tried to welcome them to the garden and ask if we could do anything for them," Zander said. He lay down and covered his face with his paws. "But as they were flying away, they were saying, 'Who are you? You're not Mother Nature!'"

I squeezed my eyes shut and cringed.

They were right. We weren't Mother Nature. We were trying to do Mother Nature's job, but we definitely weren't as good as her.

"That's okay," Zoey said. "Maybe if they come around next time when Mother Nature is awake, they'll want to talk to us then."

She was right.

"Let's go down to the White Room and work on Mother Nature's cure. Zoey continued. "That way, we won't disturb her while she's sleeping."

I looked back over at my sister resting against the tree. I still wanted to wake her up. I felt like I needed to talk to her—I had some questions about how to be Mother Nature and how we could help her feel better. But Aurelia needed to sleep.

I nodded, and the three of us walked back to the platform that would drop us down through the dirt and grass of Aurelia's garden room to the main part of the castle.

"Down!" I commanded the platform. As we sank into the ground, my heart sank in my chest.

I wiggled my fingers in a wave to my sister. It was time to get to work—without her.

CHAPTER 2

THE TUNNEL

The White Room looked exactly the same as it had before we went to see my sister. I was a little surprised. It was getting late in the day, and I thought that the castle would have been getting darker. I didn't see lights or candles anywhere, but the room was still filled with a warm, yellow light.

Uncle T was standing in the middle of the White Room looking at his watch. He's actually Father Time to the rest of the world, but since he's my uncle, I just call him Uncle T.

He glanced at us as we returned to the floor.

"Interesting hair," he said without smiling. He's too serious to smile most of the time.

My friends and I looked at each other and giggled. I had almost forgotten about our hair. Just before we went up to see Aurelia, I had tried to clean us up because we were all muddy from the flood adventure. Only I turned Zoey's dress inside out and made the flowers in her hair bigger. I also made Zander look like a fuzzy puffball. Apparently I made my hair stand tall like a tower, but I couldn't see that. I had to trust my friends when they said that's what happened.

"Do you think it's a good fashion statement?" I asked, striking a silly pose.

I didn't really think Uncle T would answer my question, but I wanted to see if I could make him smile.

He didn't.

Zoey looked in Mother Nature's purse. It was filled with tools that helped control nature, but they were disguised as everyday, normal things like makeup, a phone, and money. Since Zoey was very responsible, she was in charge of holding it.

She pulled out a hairbrush. "I know this has special Mother Nature powers," she said, "but maybe it also works like a regular brush and we can use it to make our hair go back to normal. I'll brush while we talk about curing Mother Nature."

Uncle T looked at his watch again. "I'm a little

worried about the Elements," he said.

He meant Earth, Water, Fire, and Air. Part of Mother Nature's job was to keep them under control, which was harder than it sounded. They had minds of their own and didn't always listen very well.

I studied Uncle T as Zoey began brushing my hair. "Why?" I asked.

"Because they said they wanted to help Aurelia get well. But suddenly I'm getting calls for meetings all over the world from different plants and animals. This is not normal, and I bet the Elements are behind it. Can you go check on Earth and see what they're planning? She's the most mature of all the Elements—and the easiest to talk to, so you should be able to get a straight answer from her."

I looked at my friends. We nodded.

"Hair—*and fur*—can wait," Zander said. He galloped toward the doors at the back of the room.

"No problem," I said. "We'll be right back."

Zoey and I linked arms and followed Zander who was now sitting in front of the middle door at the back of the room.

When we walked through the door, we saw Isla the white peacock sitting on her silver throne, just as she always did. Her feathers were fanned out behind her beautifully.

I stepped toward her. My friends were right next to me.

"Hi Isla," I said (her name sounded like *eye-la*). "I was wondering if I could go see Miss Earth. Is that okay?"

Isla didn't answer, but I expected that. She never answered.

"I'll take that as a *yes*," I said. I took Mother Nature's keys off my belt where I kept them and walked past Isla to another door. This time I used the green key to unlock it; I knew that key was supposed to open the door to Earth's realm.

Right behind me, Zoey said, "This is going to be fun. I can't wait to see what it's like to visit Earth. She helps so many wonderful things grow."

I swung open the door and saw nothing but darkness. Nearly complete darkness.

"What is this?" Zoey asked. Her voice had been happy and hopeful a moment before, but it wasn't anymore. It was softer and higher—with just a hint of worry.

I had to admit, I was a little nervous, too. We were facing *a lot* of darkness. My stomach felt like there were hundreds of tiny bubbles popping in it.

Zander sniffed around. "It smells like dirt. We

must be going into an underground tunnel."

More bubbles popped in my stomach. When we went to visit the Element Air, we took a stairway up to the sky. When we visited the Element Water, we took a slide down to the water. I liked the idea of stairways and slides better than underground tunnels.

"It's okay," Zander said. His voice was cheerful. "I can see in the dark. Between my awesome eagle eyes and my Golden Retriever nose, we'll find our way."

Zoey and I looked at our four-legged friend and then at each other. We smiled.

Thank goodness for Zander.

"Lead the way," I said. "But not too fast."

I took hold of Zander's tail. Zoey took my free hand. We were like a chain, and we walked slowly through the tunnel. The ground felt soft and maybe even a little damp. Every now and then my shoes would make a *squish* sound into a particularly soft spot.

Yuck, I thought. I remembered how we had to stop a flood earlier that day and all the mud involved in that adventure. I already had enough mud for one day.

"Almost there," Zander said.

Only a couple minutes had probably passed,

but it felt like a whole hour. Traveling to see Air and Water was very different—it was super-fast. This seemed super-slow. I wondered if this meant Earth's personality was a lot different from Air's and Water's personalities. Uncle T said she was more mature than the other Elements, and maybe he was right. Last time we met her, she was mad at Water for raining too much in a desert. Maybe that wasn't how she normally was—and maybe she really was less dramatic and emotional. I hoped so.

"I can smell a change in the air," Zander said. "We're almost to the end."

I heard Zoey sigh with relief. I sighed, too.

We turned a corner in the tunnel. Suddenly it filled with light. I had to squint as my eyes adjusted to the brightness.

"Let's go," Zander said.

Still squinting, I let go of my friends, and we ran toward the tunnel's end.

Once outside, we were in a small, warm meadow. It reminded me of our garden. There was a grassy clearing all around us, and further down the way was a little stream trickling by. Birds were singing happily in the trees.

"This is beautiful," Zoey said. She skipped past us and spun around with her arms held wide. "Beautiful!"

Zander ran after Zoey and then chased his tail in a circle.

It *was* beautiful. The sun was starting to set, and everything looked a little purplish.

After a moment of taking in the beauty, I remembered why we were there. It was time to take care of business. I took a deep breath and cleared my throat.

"Miss Earth?" I said. "It's me, Sarafina, Aurelia's sister. I hate to bother you, but do you have a second to talk?"

I paused. I was hoping Earth would respond.

She didn't.

"I know that you're busy," I said.

Out of the corner of my eye, I could see Zoey and Zander. They were no longer spinning and running in circles. They were walking back over to me.

"Uncle T said that he's being called into a lot of meetings," I said. "Do those meetings have to do with the Elements' plans to cure my sister?"

Zander and Zoey were almost to me. I looked at them and shrugged.

"She's not answering," I whispered.

A loud rumbling sound suddenly filled the air.

I looked at my friends. They looked back at me blankly. Then I felt it. So did they.

At the same time, we all exclaimed, "Earthquake!"

Zoey and I bent down to Zander. We huddle together in one big hug, bracing ourselves for the shaking.

CHAPTER 3

GRUMBLY, RUMBLY EARTH

The shaking and rumbling stopped just as quickly as it started. After a moment, we looked up. Before we could speak, we heard a voice all around us.

"Ah," the voice said. "That's much better."

I stood up. "Earth? Miss Earth? Is that you?"

We heard a laugh—a deep, grumbly laugh.

"Of course it's me. Who else would it be?"

Another grumbly laugh followed. The ground vibrated just a little.

"Are you okay?" I asked. "Did you just have an earthquake?"

"Oh, I did," Earth said. "I really don't like

doing that, but it sure does make me feel better. Sometimes I get so uncomfortable. You can understand, can't you? Don't you get stiff if you haven't moved in a long time? I just wish earthquakes didn't scare animals and humans so much."

I looked at my friends. I also wished earthquakes weren't so scary. They were loud, they shook everything around, and worst of all, we never knew when they were coming.

"Thanks for taking the time to talk to us," I said.

"I only have a moment," Earth said.

I thought back to the afternoon when Water was causing the flood. That was also when the Elements decided they wanted to help Mother Nature get better, and I wondered if that was why Earth didn't have a lot of time to chat at the moment.

"Do you have to get back to your meeting with Water?" I asked. "Are you still meeting to come up with a cure for Mother Nature?"

Earth vibrated, just barely.

"Oh no, that ended awhile ago," she said. "In fact, we've already begun working on the first stages of our plan."

"Wow," Zoey said. "That was really fast."

I cleared my throat. "That's great," I said. "Can you tell us what the plan is? Uncle T was—"

"I don't have time to think about that right now," Earth said. "Not with the *really* big earthquake coming."

Zoey and Zander gasped. I probably gasped, too, but I was so surprised that I wasn't paying attention to myself.

"A big one?" Zander whispered.

"What do you mean?" I asked.

"Well, down below the ocean floor, there's lava. We call it magma," Earth said. "Right now, under the Pacific Ocean, there's some magma that want to push up through the surface. That's thanks to Fire, of course. And when magma pushes through the ocean floor, I have to move over to make room for it. I'll tell you, that's not fun. When I quake underwater, it can cause a tidal wave. Then Water gets mad at me for causing problems. And then Air makes jokes because, well, Air makes jokes about everything." Earth sighed. "But it's really all Fire's fault. I wish that she and her magma would leave me alone. Enough is enough, really."

I looked at my friends. This sounded very, very complicated. And I just wanted to find out how Earth and Water planned to cure my sister. This earthquake, magma, tidal wave stuff was too much.

Also, Earth was getting a little huffy and upset. I didn't want that. What if it made her cause another earthquake? I needed to be careful with what I said next.

"I'm sorry to hear about all that," I said slowly.

Maybe I needed to change the subject. But how?

"I haven't met Fire yet," I continued. "Is she nice?"

"Nice?" Earth laughed again, rumbling a little. "She's fiery."

"Isn't she supposed to be fiery?" Zander whispered to me. "She's Fire, after all, right?"

I shrugged. I didn't know what to say.

"Oh, you'll meet her soon enough," Earth said. "Now if you'll excuse me, it's time for me to go tend to the magma problem."

"Wait!" I blurted out. "We need your help. We need to find out what your plan is to cure my sister. Can you tell us, please?"

"Sarafina, really, I don't have the time. I really need to—"

"*Pretty please*?" I interrupted her. "Can you wait just one more second and tell us what's happening? Uncle T isn't going to be happy if I come back without any information." I knew I sounded worried—maybe even a little frantic. I *felt* worried and frantic. I wasn't controlling my feelings well.

"I really must be off. And everything is just fine—it's all going according to plan. Don't worry. In the meantime, you're here to take over Mother Nature's jobs. All is well."

I shook my head. "It's not the same. I'm doing my best, but I make a lot of mistakes. And I get *really* dirty."

"There's nothing wrong with a little dirt," Earth laughed. "You are doing just fine. No one expects you to be perfect, Sarafina. Don't fret. Just do your best. And now I am off to deal with the magma. We can chat again later."

Then Earth was gone.

I looked at my friends. We had not been able to do what Uncle T asked us to do. We did not find out what the Elements were up to.

I didn't think that Uncle T was going to be very happy.

My friends must have been able to read my mind. Zander jumped up and licked my face. As gross as it was, it made me laugh.

Zoey patted my shoulder. "It's okay," she said. "Maybe we can go ask Water about the plan they came up with. Or even Air. He was trying to make the meeting, too."

I nodded.

"But before that, I have an idea," Zander said. He looked toward the little brook trickling by. "Why don't we use the water over there to help wet down our hair and fur. That will make it go back to normal."

I laughed. I had forgotten about our crazy hair.

"Good idea," Zoey said.

Zander ran off to the water. Zoey fluttered her wings and skipped quickly after him. I followed behind and tried to keep up.

While we wet down our hair, I thought about how I could tell Uncle T that we didn't get an answer. I wasn't looking forward to that.

CHAPTER 4

WELCOME TO LIFE AS MOTHER NATURE

Back at the castle, Uncle T was busy. He sat at the black table in the White Room, hunched over something. As we got closer, I could see it was a clipboard. He was writing something on a clipboard.

He did not look up, but he began talking to us. "How did it go?" he asked.

I bit my lip and scrunched up my face.

"Not so good," I answered. "Earth didn't want to talk to us. There's going to be a big earthquake, and she had to get ready for it."

Uncle T still didn't look up. He did check his

watch, but he didn't look at us. He nodded at the clipboard.

"Understood," he said. "Then you need to get ready for the earthquake as well."

My eyes grew. I looked at my friends. They looked back at me. Their eyes were also wide.

The good news was that Uncle T wasn't mad that I didn't find out about the Elements' plan. The bad news was that I had to get ready for an earthquake.

"Why?" I asked. "What do I have to do with an earthquake?"

Uncle T kept writing. "You're taking over Mother Nature's jobs. You have to keep as many people and things as safe as possible."

I slapped my forehead. Of course. How could I forget about that?

But wait—how was I going to *do* that?

I was just about to ask Uncle T when the key ring on my belt began buzzing.

"Oh, not again," I grumbled. I reached for the key ring. "Just when I find out I have to do something important, another something comes along. We're never going to get everything done."

Uncle T finally looked up. Strangely, he was smiling. Why did he decide to smile *now* of all times?

"Welcome to life as Mother Nature," he said.

Then the smile faded, and he went back to scribbling on the clipboard.

That seemed like a strange comment to make, but I didn't have time to think about it. Zoey began tugging on my arm.

"Let's go, Feenie," she said. "It's the Plant Kingdom key that's vibrating. Let's go see what the plants need."

I let Zoey lead me to the Plant Kingdom door. Zander followed.

Once we walked through the door, we were surrounded by a half-circle of trees. The first time we were there, it was morning. The sun was shining high in the sky. It was evening this time, so the sky was darker. The full moon glowed bright white above us.

"Where are we going?" I asked.

Zoey pointed to one of the trees. It was tall and nearly white. The bark was smooth. Inside the tree's trunk, a door slid open.

"That's the South America tree," Zoey said. "We're going somewhere in South America."

"Really? How do you know?" Zander asked.

Zoey smiled. "It's kind of like how you can talk to animals, Zander," she answered. "I just know."

I nodded. Truly, my friends had awesome talents.

The hollowed out space inside the tree was big enough for us to fit, even with Zoey's big wings. Once we were in there, we waited.

"What do we do now?" I asked. I touched the inside wall of the tree. It was smooth, and it didn't look like there were any buttons to push anywhere.

"I bet we need to hold on," Zander said.

Before I could ask why, the bottom of the tree seemed to drop. We were suddenly zooming downward.

"Whoa!" we cried.

I felt like my stomach had been pushed into my head. My head felt like it had been left back at the castle. We were moving so fast that I was dizzy. My eyes were blurry. Zoey and I grasped at each other's arms.

"How long is this going to take?" Zoey moaned.

"Wheee!" Zander exclaimed.

"I don't know," I called back to Zoey. I closed my eyes, trying to keep the dizziness from getting any worse. "Hopefully not much—"

Thud.

Suddenly, we stopped. I didn't even get to

finish my sentence before the ride was over. I blinked a couple times. My eyes were still a little blurry from zooming through the tree so fast.

"That was awesome," Zander said.

Zoey gave a short, weak laugh. "I don't know about that, Zander," she said. "I hope we don't have to do that every time we need to help a plant. I don't think my stomach could take it."

I shook my head. My eyes were *still* blurry. "Maybe we'll get used to it," I muttered weakly.

Slowly, the tree door slid open. We peered out. Wherever we were, it was nighttime. Immediately I knew we were in a garden—I could smell the flowers.

"I see the problem," Zoey said. She squeezed past me and Zander. She used her wings to hop quickly across the grass.

We followed. Zander had no problem keeping up—he was a Golden Retriever after all. But, as usual, I couldn't run as fast as a dog or hop as fast as a fairy with rose petal wings. I did my best, though. I didn't want to lose sight of them in the darkness.

I had no idea what Zoey had meant about a problem. Everything looked peaceful to me. No floods, no mixed-up rainbows, no strong winds— everything looked fine.

When I finally caught up, I could see Zoey hunching over a bush with interesting flowers. They were long and yellow, and they were hanging upside down. They almost looked like bells decorating the bush.

I was going to ask Zoey about them when I noticed that Zander was walking in circles sniffing the air. Either he was concentrating really hard or something was wrong—or maybe it was both. He was probably concentrating really hard on something wrong.

I stood motionless and quiet. Obviously my friends were taking charge here. It would be better for me to wait until they told me what to do.

The seconds seemed to crawl by. I really wanted to ask what was going on, but I kept quiet. *Be patient*, I told myself. *Take some deep breaths, enjoy the wonderful smell of night-blooming flowers, and just be patient.*

"I see them!" Zander exclaimed. And with that, he sprinted away.

I looked after him.

See who? I wanted to ask. *Where are you going?*
I loved having such smart, hard working friends. But sometimes they sure did confuse me.

CHAPTER 5

A BAD IDEA

Zoey turned away from the bush. Her wings fluttered just a little to help her skip quickly over to me.

"The Angel Trumpet flowers are upset," she said. She nodded over her shoulder to the yellow flowers that looked like bells. A disappointed look crossed her face.

"Why?" I asked.

Zoey sighed. "You know how there are some moths that pollinate the flowers that bloom at night?"

I nodded. I *sort of* knew that. It sounded familiar. I figured that my sister had probably told me about that a long time ago.

"There's a problem with the moths that normally pollinate the Angel Trumpets."

I crossed my arms. "Why?"

"It seems the fireflies are eating all the pollen," Zoey continued, "and not leaving anything for the moths."

My mouth dropped open. I understood why she looked disappointed.

"Why are the fireflies doing that?" I asked. "That's not okay. How do we fix this?"

Zoey turned and looked where Zander had been running. She pointed after him.

"Zander was going to find the moths and fireflies so we could work this out. While we wait, let's look through Mother Nature's purse. Maybe something in there will help calm down the Angel Trumpets. They're so upset that they're actually shaking."

Yikes. Shaking flowers couldn't be good.

I nodded and then glanced in the direction Zander had been running. I couldn't see anything in the dark. Thank goodness for that dog's incredible eagle eyes. He could see anything from a mile away—even moths at nighttime.

"I wonder if Zander can talk to moths and fireflies," I said.

Zoey shrugged. "That would be amazing." She started searching through Mother Nature's purse. "Hmm," she said under her breath. "I don't know if a mirror could do anything. No, no, no. Maybe the paint?" She pulled out the bottle of paint we had used to fix the mixed-up rainbow. She shook her head at it. "No, probably not. A comb? No. What about some perfume?"

A memory popped into my mind.

"I know about that perfume bottle," I said. "I remember from when I was a little girl and Uncle T was testing me for Mother Nature's talents. I'm pretty sure it's used to give plants and animals the right scent—"

I gasped as an idea came to me.

"Maybe the Angel Trumpets need their scent to be refreshed. Maybe the scent isn't strong enough, and that's causing the moths and fireflies to get confused about what they're supposed to do. Since Mother Nature has been sick, no one's been checking on things like this."

Zoey looked at the Angel Trumpets and bit her lip. Softly, she said, "I think they smell fine, Feenie. When I was talking to them, they didn't say anything about needing more scent."

Before I could respond, I heard Zander's voice.

"Found them!"

He skidded to a stop just a couple feet from us. Hovering all around his head was a cloud fireflies and moths. There must have been hundreds of them. Thousands, maybe. I had never seen so many at one time. The fireflies glowed red, yellow, and green, making the cloud look like an enormous, bright night-light. Zoey and I shaded our eyes.

"Good!" I said. "Let's get this taken care of. I have a great plan."

"Zander, can you talk to the moths and fireflies?" Zoey asked.

Zander nodded. "Yep, I sure can. Can you believe it? I think I might be able to talk to all animals." He laughed his beautiful dolphin laugh.

"That's great," I said. "You talk to them about what's going on. I'm going to try something here." I held out my hand toward Zoey, and she gave me the perfume bottle, hesitating just a little. Then Zoey bent down to talk to Zander. They must have been sharing stories about what the flowers and the insects had told each of them.

I looked at the bottle. It was made of heavy glass and had a pretty bulb that needed to be squeezed to spray the perfume. To myself, I said *let's hope this works.*

Then I walked over to the Angel Trumpet bush and held the perfume bottle close to it.

"Wait!" Zoey and Zander exclaimed, suddenly breaking from the huddle. "Wait—that's not the answer!"

But it was too late. I had already sprayed the bush.

"Oh no!" I gasped as soon as I smelled what had come from the perfume bottle.

It smelled like skunk.

Suddenly the flowers weren't just shaking a little. They were shaking a lot. They may have been upset before about the fireflies, but now they were *angry*. And I was pretty sure they were angry at me.

Zoey ran over to them and, plugging her nose, started muttering something in flower-language. Her voice sounded almost like the wind.

The fireflies and moths scattered, and the night-light that had been brightening the garden disappeared.

"Wait!" Zander howled. He ran around in circles as though trying to chase all the insects at one. "Come back! We need to talk!"

I dropped the perfume bottle into my pocket and plugged my nose. With my other hand, I covered my eyes. I shook my head.

What have I done? I asked myself.

Zoey said that the flowers smelled right. Why hadn't I just listened to her?

CHAPTER 6

A BETTER IDEA

Zoey turned to me. Then she pointed to a couple Angel Trumpet flowers that had fallen off the bush earlier.

"Help me pick those up," she said with her nose still plugged. Her voice sounded a little muffled, almost like she had a cold, but I heard her just fine. "Those ones didn't get sprayed. We can fix this with their help."

"How?" I asked, scrambling to pick up as many flowers as I could while still holding my nose with one hand.

"They're Angel *Trumpets*," Zoey said. "If we give them a command and then blow into them like a trumpet, they'll send the message to the other flowers."

My mouth dropped open. I had never heard of that. Ever. "How do you know?"

"The flowers on the bush told me. I don't know why it would work—if it *does* work in the first place—but it's worth trying." She unplugged her nose and took a deep breath through her mouth. Then she said into the small end of the flower, "Blow away the skunk smell, please." She pointed the Angel Trumpet at the bush and blew.

I copied my friend. After we each blew through one flower, we laid it down and then used a different flower to do the same thing.

I took a tiny breath through my nose. The skunk smell didn't seem as strong.

"I think it's working," I said.

Zoey nodded as she brought another Angel Trumpet toward her face. "I think so, too. Keep going."

We worked hard, flower after flower, until all the flowers that had been on the ground were used.

I felt out of breath and my heart was beating faster than normal, but I hoped all the hard work had paid off.

I crossed my fingers and took a deep breath,

testing the smell of the air.

"I still smell a little skunk," I said.

Zoey looked at the Angel Trumpet bush and listened for a moment. Then she turned toward me and smiled.

"The flowers say they've been fix," she said. "I think the only thing that still smells like skunk here is you." She patted my shoulder.

I didn't really like smelling like skunk, but what bothered me more was my mistake. This had been all my fault. I should have just listened to Zoey in the first place. I should have let my friends handle this one.

Zoey patted my shoulder again. "It's okay, Feenie," she said. "You fixed the problem."

"No, you fixed the problem. I caused it."

Zoey smiled kindly. "We all make mistakes. What's important is that we learn from them. And in this case, we fixed the mistake."

"Whaa-hoooo!" Zander said, running full speed over to us. He skidded to a stop just a foot away and sat back on his haunches.

"That was crazy," he laughed. "I don't think the fireflies will want to bother the Angel Trumpets any time soon now."

I closed my eyes and shook my head. *That was not fun,* I thought to myself.

It was time to change the subject.

"Zander, why were the fireflies eating all the pollen?" I asked.

"Oh, they were bored. Can you imagine that? What a silly excuse. But it's okay now. I talked to them and taught them a new game so they won't get bored again, and they understand they can't take over the moth's territory. We have it all worked out." He laughed his dolphin laugh.

Zoey bent down and began picking up the Angel Trumpet flowers we had used to blow away the skunk smell.

"Let's take these back with us to the castle. We can put them in a vase in the White Room for decoration."

I nodded and helped pick up the flowers. It was a good idea; maybe it would even cheer me up.

Once we had all the flowers, we walked back to our special tree.

The ride home didn't seem as scary. This time, we knew what we were getting ourselves into. My stomach still felt like it was back by the Angel Trumpets, even after we got home, and my eyes were blurry again. But still, it wasn't as bad as the first time. Bracing ourselves before the ride definitely helped.

Uncle T wasn't in the White Room when we got back to the castle. We walked straight to the black table and dropped all the Angel Trumpets on it. Zoey dug through Mother Nature's purse and pulled out a tall, blue vase. She set it on the table.

"I didn't know there was a vase in the purse," I said, feeling amazed.

Zoey smiled. "Mother Nature is prepared for anything." She went to work arranging the flowers in the vase. When she was done, there was one Angel Trumpet left over that didn't fit. She put it in Mother Nature's purse—probably for safe keeping.

"What do you think?" she asked me and Zander, smiling. Her eyes were green with little flecks of yellow in them, almost matching the yellow Angel Trumpets.

Before we could answer, a warm breeze filled the castle. We looked around, wondering where it came from. Warm breezes in the middle of the night—and in a castle—how strange! Then I remembered what happened after we painted the rainbow on the wall of the castle that morning. And I remembered what happened after we put our muddy prints on the wall that afternoon. The light had changed from a bright white to a warm yellow. Uncle T had said the castle liked having us there. Maybe the warm breeze was saying the same.

"The castle loves it," I said. "You brought some warmth in."

We admired the beautiful Angel Trumpet arrangement. After a moment, Zoey said, "It's incredible how these flowers were able to fix the skunk smell. It makes me wonder what powers other plants have. I wonder if animals have powers, too."

I thought about what Zoey said and agreed. It was incredible how powerful the plants were. And like she said, animals probably had pretty amazing abilities as well.

It reminded me of how Water and Earth were having meetings with the plants and animals to find a cure for my sister. I wondered if they had come up with anything just yet.

Uncle T walked into the room. He was holding a clipboard and writing fast. *Really fast.* His hand looked like it was almost smoking from how fast it was zooming across the paper.

He didn't look up at us. Still writing, he said, "I was hoping that everything went well with your trip to help the flowers in South America. From the smell of things, that might not be what happened."

Zoey smiled at me. Zander did too—as much as a dog can smile, that is.

"It all worked out," Zoey said.

Uncle T kept writing. He nodded and said, "Then the details don't really matter. As long as everything is fine."

"Can you help us learn to use Mother Nature's tools correctly?" I asked my uncle while pointing to the purse that Zoey had strapped across her chest. "There's still so much that we don't know about. Like the perfume bottle. How do we use that?"

Uncle T shook his head. "It just takes practice. Perhaps you'll have time to practice sometime soon."

My belt vibrated. I looked down and saw the green key on my belt loop buzzing.

"Looks like Earth needs us," I said.

Uncle T sat down at the table, still scribbling on his clipboard. "You better get going then. While you are there, if Water shows up, ask her to help you get rid of that skunk smell."

My spirits rose a little bit. Water could help with the skunk smell? That would be awesome.

"Will do," I called over my shoulder as I raced to Isla's door.

Zoey and Zander were right behind me.

CHAPTER 7

TIME TO BOUNCE

One of Isla's feathers was glowing a bright white, and as I neared the peacock, I could see a picture of a small island. Although it was still nighttime, I could tell that the island was covered in small houses across a hillside.

"That must be where the earthquake is going to happen," I said. "That's what Earth said she was worried about. Remember? Magma was pushing up through the ocean floor, and then Earth was going to have to shift to get comfortable again."

We ran for the door that would take us to the island.

"Will we be able to get there fast enough?" Zoey asked as I used the green key to unlocked the door and threw it open.

I knew exactly what Zoey meant. The last time we went through Earth's tunnel, it was so dark that we couldn't move very fast.

"I'll get us there," Zander said. "Just hang onto my tail, and we'll go as fast as we can."

We did just as Zander said. Holding his tail, we moved quickly through the dark, dank, earthen tunnel. There was no time to worry about falling. Plus we knew we could trust Zander.

I wondered what we possibly could do about an earthquake. I thought about all the tools in Mother Nature's purse. The mirror, the brush, the coins, the paint, and, what else? I couldn't remember anything else. None of those things seemed like they would be very helpful, and we still didn't know how to use most of them anyway.

The last bit of Earth's tunnel turned into a steep slope, and we had to use our hands to climb upward. I could only tell that we were close to the end because of the moonlight shining through the opening. For a moment, I almost felt like we were digging ourselves out of a hole.

Finally, we pulled ourselves through the last bit of tunnel and found ourselves on the island pictured in Isla's feather. We were right at the edge of where the sandy beach met the grass and palm trees.

I looked toward the ocean. The whole beach was deserted. There were only a couple palm trees here and there across the whole sandy area.

I turned around. Beyond the beach were rolling hills. Scattered across the hills were little white houses. There weren't any street lamps among the houses, but the full moon was bright enough to help us see them.

Humans lived there. If we didn't help protect them during the earthquake, there could be trouble.

"Miss Earth?" I called. The roar of the ocean waves behind us was loud, so I had to be louder. "Miss Earth, how are you doing? We got your call. Are you feeling okay?"

A voice all around us groaned. I thought I might have felt the ground vibrate a little, but I told myself that was just my imagination.

"I need to stretch," Earth said. "It happened, just like I said it would. Fire made the magma push through, and I can't stand it anymore. I'm so uncomfortable now—I need to adjust!"

Now? I wondered. I grabbed my friends and huddled with them, ready for the earthquake to hit.

"Okay," I called out to Earth as we still braced ourselves for shaking. "Can you do it just a little at a time, sort of slowly so that the people on this island won't feel it?"

"I don't know," Earth moaned. "I'm worried that I might break some of these houses. They're old, and they aren't sturdy. Help me, please!"

"How?" I asked. "How can I help you? What would Mother Nature do?"

Earth groaned again. "I can't take it anymore!"

A sudden gust of wind rushed by, and I knew we had a visitor.

"Air!" I exclaimed. "What are you doing here?"

"I heard you might be having a little trouble," Air said. "What can I do to help?"

I looked at my friends. We loosened our grip on each other just a little.

"I don't know," I said. "What should we do?"

"Oh, *Feenie*," Air said dramatically, "Why don't you just change the ground so that it won't shake as much?"

"How do I do that?" I asked.

Earth groaned again. "Oh, how I hate when lava seeps through the ocean floor," she lamented.

"Just use your mind," Air said. "Like you always do. Concentrate."

"What?" I said. "Whenever I try to do that, I make things worse! That's why I smell like—"

I stopped talking abruptly. It hit me—when I sprayed the Angel Trumpet flowers with the perfume earlier, I didn't concentrate on making sure the perfume had the right scent. I just sprayed without thinking. Maybe if I had concentrated, I wouldn't have sprayed them with skunk smell, and I wouldn't smell like a skunk myself.

"Oh," I groaned, smacking my forehead with my palm.

But there was no time to think about that now.

Air laughed with another gust. "Well, it is true that you make mistakes. But it's always fun to watch."

Zoey squeezed my arm. "Just concentrate," she said to me. "You don't always make things worse. You can do it."

Zander barked in agreement.

I had to try. If I concentrated this time, at least I had a better chance of fixing the problem than when I didn't concentrate at all with the Angel Trumpets. I closed my eyes.

Concentrate, I told myself. *Make the ground soft so no one will get hurt.*

Suddenly, the sandy dirt we were standing on between the beach and the grass seemed to change. It felt squishy and even a little bouncy. I tried to take a step forward, but instead I sank down and bounced up.

"Did you do it?" Zander asked. "Is this what will keep the earthquake from causing damage to those houses?"

I shrugged. Then I smiled. "Maybe I did." I tried to take another step and the same thing happened—I sunk down and then bounced up. Sand flew into the air alongside me. It was like a trampoline. Imagine that—a whole island being built on a trampoline!

"I figured if the ground was soft, no one would get hurt, right? Soft things don't hurt." I tried making myself bounce a little higher. "Hey, this is fun," I said. "Zoey, is this what you feel like when you're flying?"

Zoey laughed. She stepped down and then fluttered her wings so that when she bounced back up, she could fly a little higher.

"This *is* fun!" she said. "And maybe when the earthquake comes, no one will feel it because the soft earth will absorb the shaking.

Earth groaned. "Oh, no," she said. "That's not right at all!"

Air laughed. The gust nearly knocked me off balance. I didn't have a solid footing now that the ground was like a trampoline. Sand flew in my face, and I used the backs of my hands to wipe it from my mouth.

"Oh Feenie, good try," Air said, "but that definitely won't work. If you are bouncing around right now when you should be standing still, imagine what will happen when the ground starts to shake. It'll just make the bouncing ten times worse! Think about it. Soft things wiggle and jiggle way more than hard things, don't they?"

My friends and I looked at each other with fear in our eyes.

"We have to do something!" I said. "How do we fix this?"

CHAPTER 8

HOLD STILL, PLEASE!

"I can't hold on much longer," Earth said. "Do something, quick!"

Air sighed. "The good thing is that everyone in town is asleep right now," he said. "No one even knows that you've made the ground bouncy. But if you don't change it quickly, they certainly will know once the ground begins quaking."

I turned toward my friends. I tried to jump over to them, but I still didn't really have my balance. I stumbled, fell to the ground, and scrambled on all fours over to Zoey and Zander.

"I can't try concentrating again to fix this," I said. "I'll just mess it up again." I turned to Zoey.

"What do we have in Mother Nature's purse? There's got to be something to help us here."

Zoey opened Mother Nature's purse and began digging through it.

"I can't see!" she said. "It's so dark outside, and the moon isn't bright enough to help me see into the purse—I just can't tell what we've got here."

"Dump everything out," I said. I was getting more nervous by the second. There wasn't going to be enough time.

"I don't think that's a good idea," Zoey said, shaking her head at the purse. "Everything will get sandy and dirty, and we still haven't learned about all the tools in here. What if something drops on the ground and explodes?"

I hadn't thought about that. Zoey was right.

"Let me help," Zander said. He ran around in a circle, managing to stay more balanced than I could on the bouncy ground. Then opened his mouth as if to speak, but no sound seemed to come out.

Zoey stopped digging through the purse and stared at Zander. Then she leaned into me and whispered, "What is he doing?"

I didn't know—but there was no time to say so.

Suddenly, a cloud of glowing fireflies swarmed around us. The insects were glowing all different colors—red, green, and yellow. They hovered just overhead, lighting the ground in a bright, beautiful way.

"I called for them," Zander said. "Now that I know how to talk to fireflies, I just asked them to come help. And here they are." He laughed. "Mother Nature's flashlight!"

Then something amazing happened. Zander's nose started glowing, just like one of the fireflies. It was bright green. I couldn't believe my eyes.

"Zander!" I squealed. "What happened? Your nose!"

He crossed his eyes, trying to get a look at it. "Ha, HA!" he laughed. "I've got a firefly nose. Quick, Zoey, use the light to look through the purse!"

Zoey's eyes were wide, and her mouth was hanging open. She was as surprised as I was about Zander's nose. But she snapped out of it quickly and went back to searching Mother Nature's purse.

"Wait," she said. "I hear something. There's something in the purse trying to talk to us."

Zoey pulled out the Angel Trumpet flower and held it up.

For the second time in the last ten second, I couldn't believe my eyes. Could the flower help us? I remembered that Zoey had put it in Mother Nature's purse right before we answered Earth's call—but how could it help us?

Zoey brought the Angel Trumpet to her ear and listened. Then her face brightened.

"The Angel Trumpet says she can help," Zoey said. "Remember how we used the flowers to blow the skunk smell away earlier this evening? She might be able to do something like that to fix this problem."

My heart felt like it skipped a beat.

"How?" I asked.

"We just have to tell her what we need to happen. Then she'll blow the announcement into the ground for us."

I held my breath as Zoey paused and listened to the flower one more time. Her face lit up again.

"We'll tell her that the ground needs to be super-hard, then we'll bury her. She'll tell the soil what we said. She thinks that once she makes the announcement, all the plant roots will hear, and they'll help spread the word—they'll help the ground harden."

"Let's do it," I said. "Tell her we need the ground as hard as a rock. That's the only way to brace for the earthquake."

"Ohhhh!" Earth groaned. "Not… much…longer…!"

Zoey hastily whispered to the flower. When she looked up, she said, "We need to bury it."

"What can we use to dig?" I asked. "Zoey, quick, what's in Mother Nature's purse?"

A gust of wind blew by us.

"Oh, Feenie, really?" Air laughed. "You're going to look in the purse for something to dig? *Think!*"

"That's right," Zander said. "I'm right here to help. What do dogs do best?"

At the same time, Zander and Air sang out, "Dig!"

I gasped. Of course!

"Over there," I said, pointing to the closest palm tree. "That will put you right next to some roots."

Zander ran to the tree and immediately started scrapping his front paws against the dirty sand next to it. Zoey and I followed, bouncing as carefully and quickly as possible. Zander's glowing nose was a perfect light to help him see what he was doing. Dirt and sand flew everywhere as he furiously scraped away. Some of it landed on my arms and dress, but I barely noticed.

"About ten seconds!" Earth warned.

"Now!" I yelled.

Zoey and I bounced to Zander and threw the Angel Trumpet into the hole. We covered it with the dirty sand as fast as we could.

"Is it working?" I asked breathlessly. "Zoey can you hear it? Is the Angel Trumpet talking to the palm tree's roots?"

Zoey put her ear to the ground. "I can't—"

"Hold onto your hats!" Earth yelled.

A loud rumbling sound filled my ears, and I reached for my friends. The ground underneath us was still squishy. The earthquake was coming, and *the earth was still squishy*. The plan hadn't worked.

We held on tightly to each other, squeezing our eyes shut.

"Here it comes!" I said.

But then, suddenly the rumbling stopped. Nothing was shaking. All was quiet. And still.

I opened my eyes and realized the ground was hard beneath my feet—I was no longer sinking into it. I looked at my friends. They looked back at me. We all looked confused, like we didn't know what had happened.

"Ah, that's so much better," Earth said. "Finally, that horrible pain is gone." She rumbled a little laugh. "I'm going to have to talk to Fire about those magma releases. I'm getting too old to keep doing it her way. There's got to be another way that doesn't bother me so much."

"Well, don't try to talk with Fire any time soon," Air said. "She's really worked up over in Hawaii. I think the big volcano is going to blow pretty soon. And I mean *really* blow. Not with just a little lava. I mean a *lot* of lava spewing everywhere, in every direction and high into the sky."

I was just beginning to feel relieved that the earthquake hadn't even felt like an earthquake and that it hadn't destroyed the houses when I realized what Air was saying. There was no time to feel relieved when a volcano was about to blow.

"What do you mean?" I asked. "What volcano?" I tried not to sound scared, but I could tell my voice was higher than normal. Volcanoes didn't sound fun to me.

"The volcano called Kilauea, of course," Air said. "Oh, it's not going to be tonight, Sarafina. Don't worry." He paused. "But I *might* have told Fire that I thought she was losing her touch. I *might* have *possibly* dared her to do something big that people wouldn't forget for a long time. That *might* be why Kilauea could erupt soon. I don't know for sure, but, you know, *maybe* that's what happened."

"Air!" Zoey, Zander, Earth, and I said all at one time.

"I know, I know!" Air said. "I really shouldn't tease her like that. *I know!* I'll try to be better. I promise. How's this: you three friends ought to go home and get some rest. I'll make sure that none of the Elements bother you the rest of the night, all right? I'll see if I can convince Fire that I was wrong. I'll tell her that she's as fierce and mighty as she's always been and that she doesn't need to make anything erupt. At least until tomorrow, okay?"

I was too tired to argue or remind Air that *he* was the one who caused most of the problems, so keeping the other Elements in line might not make that big of a difference. So instead, I just nodded.

"Let's go back," I said.

I looked at my friends. Zoey looked tired. She was trying to rub her eyes without getting any dirty sand in them. Zander's nose wasn't glowing anymore.

As my friends and I turned toward the tunnel leading to the castle, Earth spoke.

"Thank you," she said. "You three are wonderful. Just wonderful. You're living up to Mother Nature's good name."

I looked at my friends and smiled. "Thank you," I said.

I hoped my friends knew I wasn't just thanking Earth. I was thanking them, too.

CHAPTER 9

LOVEY DOVEY

When we got back to Isla's room, Uncle T was standing next to the peacock's silvery throne waiting for us.

"Hi Uncle T," I said. "How are you doing? You look busy."

And he did look busy. He was scribbling notes on that same clipboard he had earlier. He looked up for a split second, and then he looked back at the clipboard.

"You're dirty again. And you still smell like skunk," he said.

I cringed. Water hadn't shown up during the earthquake, so I couldn't ask for her help. And

Uncle T was right about being dirty again. I looked at my dress. It was smudged with dirt everywhere. My arms didn't look any better. Burying that Angel Trumpet had been messy.

"Sorry," I said.

Uncle T turned and walked into the White Room, still writing. We followed.

"Don't be sorry," he said. "Just take care of it whenever you can. Hopefully sooner than later— for your own sake. I doubt you enjoy smelling like skunk."

I thought Uncle T would sit at the table, but he didn't. He stood next to it. He checked his watch and then went back to writing.

"What are you doing?" I asked him.

"Taking messages," Uncle T said. He shook his head at the clipboard. "I still don't know what Earth and Water told the plants and animals in their meeting, but it seems like every living thing has a suggestion to help cure Mother Nature. They're calling me into endless meetings to take notes. They want me to pass the ideas on to Aurelia so that she can decide whether she wants to try any of them."

He took a stack of papers off the clipboard and handed it to me.

"Can you take these messages to your sister?"

he asked. "These are all the suggestions so far. Please see if she wants to read them."

I nodded at the stack. It was thick and heavy. The writing on the top page was small and scribbly. I didn't recognize the words. It probably was a language I didn't know.

"I've got to get back to taking messages," Uncle T said, "but good job with Earth this evening. You helped avoid quite a disaster."

Before I could answer, Uncle T walked toward the Animal Kingdom door and disappeared through it.

I looked at my friends. "It's a good thing he doesn't get tired or slow down. He's got a big job."

I walked to the table and was about to tap its edge so that it could become an elevator when Zoey said, "Wait!"

Zander and I turned toward our fairy friend.

"Let's see if you can use your mind to get to Mother Nature's room. The more you practice, the better you'll get."

I nodded. I held out my hand toward Zoey and then placed my other hand on Zander's head. Then I closed my eyes and concentrated really hard.

Take us to Aurelia's room, I said to myself.

Nothing happened.

Take us to Aurelia's room please, I thought again.

But again, nothing happened.

I opened my eyes.

"I can't do it yet," I said.

Zander jumped up and licked my face. "That's okay," he said. "You'll be able to do it soon."

Zoey smiled at me. "You just have to keep trying," she said. "Right now, you've got to be exhausted from the long day. Maybe when you're not so tired it will be easier."

I nodded. And then we rode up to my sister's room on our handy-dandy table elevator.

After we rose through the dirt and grass, I looked around for my sister. She wasn't sleeping against the big tree like she normally was. She wasn't sitting under any tree, actually.

"Where is she?" I asked under my breath.

Zoey and Zander looked around with me.

"I'm up here," Aurelia said.

I turned toward the sound of my sister's voice. I could tell it was coming from a distance—but I wasn't sure exactly where.

"Aurelia? Where are you?" I called.

"In the doves' tree."

"I know," Zander said. He broke into a run. Zoey fluttered her wings and half-flew, half-skipped after Zander. I tried to keep up the best I could.

When Zander stopped at the foot of the tree with beautiful white and purple flowers, I still couldn't find my sister. I spun around, looking.

"Up here," Aurelia said.

We looked up and saw my sister sitting on a tree branch in between two brown doves.

"What are you doing up there?" I asked. "Are you feeling better?"

Aurelia stroked the top of the birds' heads and then disappeared. The birds flew away, and then Aurelia reappeared standing next to me.

"What were you doing up there?" I asked.

My sister smiled. "The doves have been bringing me get-well wishes," she said. "Doves have been coming in and out all day to share warm thoughts from plants and animals everywhere."

My friends and I looked at each other knowingly.

"Ah!" we said together.

"That's why there were doves in the garden the last time we visited," I said.

Doves were messenger birds, after all. It made perfect sense that they would be the ones to bring my sister get-well wishes.

Aurelia put her hand on my shoulder. "Let's sit

down," she said.

I could tell she was tired, probably from visiting with the doves. I helped my sister sit down under the tree. Zander and Zoey found Aurelia's flower blanket and laid it across her lap.

I held up the stack of papers that Uncle T had given me. "I've also got all these messages for you. They're ideas from plants and animals about how to make you feel better."

Aurelia closed her eyes and nodded. "That's so kind of them. And it's kind of Uncle T to take notes." She opened her eyes. "Thanks for bringing the messages to me."

I nodded.

Then Aurelia continued talking. "Every plant and every animal has a secret about life, you know. They all see the world differently, and they all have different talents. Now they're trying to share their talents—*their secrets*—to help me."

Aurelia took a deep breath and tried to smile.

"Just like how the Angel Trumpet helped you harden the ground," she went on. "That kind of flower can send messages like a trumpet—and that's the Angel Trumpet's secret experience in life. A lot of living things want to share their secrets, but they don't know how. Right now, they're all seeing my illness as a chance to help and share what they can do."

I held out the stack of messages. "Would you like to see what they've all said?"

Aurelia shook her head. "I'm too tired right now. I'm sorry."

Zoey nudged me. Then she leaned in and whispered, "Maybe we can go through the messages and try out the different ideas for her. I bet we can figure out how to read Uncle T's scribbly handwriting pretty quickly."

I nodded slowly at first, but soon the nods were quite fast. The wheels in my head were turning.

"Can we stay up here in the garden and read through the messages for you?" I asked Aurelia.

She nodded. "Of course. But you also need to sleep first. You haven't had any time to rest for quite awhile."

I looked at my friends. We were dirty from head to toe and pretty worn out after the long day.

"Stay here tonight," Aurelia continued. "Ask Water to send a shower so that you can get cleaned up, and then make yourselves at home. You'll have more time to sleep if you stay here."

My friends and I looked at each other and nodded.

"And Zoey, when the rain comes, be sure to

practice your dancing," Aurelia said. "You're going to need it soon. And Zander, keep practicing your languages. Remember what it felt like when your nose turned into a firefly. Remember that feeling, and whatever you do, follow your instincts."

Zoey and Zander looked at each other. Then they nodded at Aurelia.

"Sarafina, call for Water," Aurelia said.

I nodded. I closed my eyes and thought, *Miss Water, can you send us a rain shower, please?*

Within a few moments, warm drops began falling from the sky.

Zoey and Zander ran in the direction of the beach, away from the trees, and danced through the rain.

I watched them and smiled.

We had our work cut out for us. I knew that finding a cure for Mother Nature was going to be hard, but it was turning out to be harder than I thought.

Controlling the Elements wasn't getting any easier, especially with Air's rascally ways. The Plant and Animal Kingdoms were a challenge, too.

I glanced at my sister. Then I looked at my friends dancing and running in the rain.
The challenge was worth it. They were all worth it.

Sarafina and

the Bubbly Volcano

by Jen Carter

CHAPTER 1

GOOFY GLASSES

"Coo! Coo! Coo!"

I opened my eyes. They were blurry from sleeping, so I blinked a couple times and rubbed them.

"Coo! Coo! Coo!"

What was that sound? Where was I?

I sat up on my bed of soft grass and looked up. Doves were singing in the trees.

"Coo! Coo! Coo!"

Really, where was I? It looked like my garden, but it didn't exactly seem like my garden.

"Good morning sleepyhead!"

I turned to my fairy friend Zoey who was talking to me. She was sitting just a couple feet away, smiling at me. Next to Zoey sat our other best friend, a big, happy, talking Golden Retriever named Zander. I was glad to see them.

Suddenly I remembered. Yesterday my sister Aurelia—who happened to be Mother Nature—got sick. I had to take over her job. Last night my friends and I were too tired to go back home to our garden, so we stayed in Mother Nature's castle—in her room actually, which was enchanted to look just like the garden where Zoey, Zander, and I lived.

Of course. Silly me for forgetting.

"Coo! Coo! Coo!"

"Why are those birds so loud?" I said with a yawn. I leaned against a tree trunk and stretched my arms over my head. I heard my friends giggle.

"Because they're bringing Mother Nature get-well messages," Zander said. Despite being a dog, he could speak like a human, so Zoey and I had no trouble understanding him. In fact, we just found out that Zander could speak like all animals. Most of the time, he stuck with his human voice, though.

I smiled. "Oh, right," I said. "Now I remember." I glanced over at Aurelia. She was sleeping under a tree not too far away. She had been spending most of her time sleeping lately, but doves were coming to bring her get-well messages from plants and animals all over the world—even when she was sleeping.

As I watched my sister, I thought, *Maybe today we can find a cure for you, Aurelia. That's what we're trying to do.*

I looked back at my friends. Something was different. What was it? Zander's fur was still golden. Zoey's hair still had flowers weaved into it, and her wings were still made of pink rose petals. That was all the same as usual.

I rubbed my eyes and looked again. My eyebrows furrowed.

"Uh, Zoey?" I asked slowly. "What are you wearing on your face?"

Again, Zoey and Zander giggled. Then Zoey took off the glasses she had been wearing. She held them toward me.

"These were in Aurelia's purse," she explained. "I found them in a little side pocket. I thought they might be reading glasses. And guess what? They are."

I took the glasses and studied them. The glass was constantly changing colors—blue to pink to yellow to green. And the rims around the glasses were thick and silvery—so silvery that looking at them almost hurt my eyes.

"Remember how Uncle T gave us that big stack of messages for Mother Nature?" Zander asked. "And remember how we couldn't read his scribbly handwriting?"

I nodded and thought about the night before. My uncle—Father Time to the rest of the world—had been taking messages from plants and animals about ideas to help Mother Nature feel better. My friends and I had taken the messages to Aurelia and were going to read through them for her. Unfortunately, we hadn't been able understand Uncle T's scribbly handwriting.

"Well," Zander continued, "put on the glasses." With his mouth, he picked up some papers on the grass and brought them to me. He dropped them in my lap. "Now you'll be able to read Uncle T's notes."

I put on the glasses. Suddenly swirls of sparkly rainbows filled my sight. I closed my eyes, feeling a little confused and dizzy.

"Whoa," I said.

"It feels a little strange at first," Zoey said, "but look at Uncle T's notes."

Slowly, oh-so-slowly, I opened my eyes so that I could see the papers on my lap.

"Ah!" I exclaimed. "Oh my goodness—wow!"

Uncle T's writing had transformed from tiny black scribbles to pictures. On the top page was a colorful scene from a jungle. Two monkeys were swinging from the branches and talking up a storm. I could hear their happy monkey voices in my ears. I didn't know what they were saying, but their chatter sounded pretty excited to me.

I flipped the page. A field of orange flowers was swaying in the wind. The sky was blue, and the sun was shining. All I could hear was the breeze blowing by.

"Coo! Coo! Coo!"

The doves were still singing in the trees above me, but I tried not to listen. I wanted to focus on Uncle T's notes.

The next page pictured a giant sequoia tree. It was so big that a tunnel had been cut through its trunk so that cars could zoom through it on the road they were taking. The page was completely silent.

I looked at my friends and took off the glasses. "This is amazing."

Zoey and Zander looked at each other and smiled.

"And we can understand what the plants and animals are saying in the pictures when we wear the glasses," Zander said.

He wagged his tail. His tongue hung out the side of his mouth. He was pretty excited.

I smiled.

"That's fantastic!" I said. "I'm glad to hear that because *I* can't understand anything they're saying."

I kept smiling. I was getting used to relying on my friends to help with Mother Nature's jobs. They could do so much that I couldn't when it came to plants and animals.

"Put the glasses on me," Zander said. "Watch!"

I did as Zander asked. I had never seen a Golden Retriever wear glasses before. It was quite a snazzy fashion statement.

"See, let me tell you what these monkeys are saying—" Zander began.

But before he could finish his sentence, something on my belt buzzed.

"Oh!" I yelped.

It was the key ring that I kept with me all the time. The keys vibrated whenever there was a Mother Nature job to do.

My heart sank. I wanted to find out what the monkeys were saying.

"Who is it?" Zoey asked. She could see me looking at the keys on my belt.

Eek! I thought once I saw which key was vibrating. It was red.

"Fire." I winced. "It's the Element Fire."

One of my jobs filling in for Mother Nature was to help control the four Elements: Air, Water, Earth, and Fire. So far, we had gotten to know a little bit about three of them. Air was rascally. Water was weepy. Earth was happy as long as none of the other Elements bothered her.

We hadn't met Fire yet. I had been worried about this one.

Fire, I said to myself. *Hot, burning, wild fire.*

Yikes.

Zander put his head to the ground and let the glasses slip off his face. "Let's do this," he said. "Time to go meet Fire!"

I took a deep breath and nodded. Zander was right. We couldn't put it off any longer.

CHAPTER 2

TRAVELING IN STYLE

My friends and I left Mother Nature's room the same way we always did: by sinking down through the enchanted garden's ground on a platform. It took us straight into the White Room, where it acted as the main table where we sat for meetings. From there, we ran into one of the three doors at the back of the room—the middle one, actually. It was the door leading to the Elements' control room.

In the center of the control room sat Isla, the white peacock whose feathers helped us find out how we were needed. She was sitting on her silver throne, looking like a queen with her feathers fanned out behind her. I scanned the feathers, looking for a glowing one. That's how we always knew what was needed; one of the feathers would glow, and a picture of the problem would appear in the circle at the end of the feather.

But no feathers were glowing.

"What's going on?" I asked. I turned toward my friends and saw that they had the same worried look in their eyes. "I thought Fire needed us. Right?"

"Oh!" Zander yelped. "I see it now—look! There's a feather on the floor." He started trotting toward Isla. "It's halfway hidden behind the throne."

Zoey and I followed. Zander was right; halfway behind Isla's throne was a long, thin, lacey feather. It glowed bright white, and at the end, a volcano was pictured. White smoke was coming out of the volcano's crater. It seemed to say to me, *yep, that's right; I'm a smoking volcano.*

I gulped. Zoey linked her arm in mine and squeezed it. She could tell I was nervous. I had been dreading this moment.

"Well, we knew this was coming," Zander sighed. "It's volcano time."

I bent down toward the feather, and Zoey bent down with me, still holding on tight.

"I wonder how the feather fell," I said.

I reached out to pick it up. Once my fingers closed around the shaft, which felt like a stiff drinking straw, it flew into the air, pulling Zoey and me with it.

"Whoa!" we yelled. My hand suddenly felt like it was glued to the feather, and it was flying right toward the door leading to Fire's world—but the door wasn't even open.

"Wait for me!" Zander yelled. He ran at full speed and leaped as high as he could—landing right on Zoey's shoulders.

"Yikes!" I screamed. "We're going to slam into the *dooooooor*!"

"I can't see!" Zoey wailed. "Zander is covering my eyes!"

"You don't want to see what's about to happen!" Zander wailed back.

The door looked like it was growing bigger and bigger as we flew toward it. I squeezed my eyes shut. I was trying to let go of the feather, but I couldn't. I was certain my palm was glued to it.

"Ahhhh!" we all yelled.

At the very last second, the door swung open and we zoomed through.

Suddenly, we were surrounded by beautiful blue sky. Warm air whipped across my face. It tangled my red hair and blurred my vision. I tried to keep my eyes open, but between the wind and my hair, I couldn't really see no matter what I did.

"Where are we going?" Zander yelled.

I could barely hear him because the wind was so loud in my ears.

"Your paw is squishing my nose!" Zoey yelled. She sounded muffled under Zander's paw. "Can you please move it?"

"I wish I could!" Zander answered. There's nowhere else for me to put *itttt*!"

"Wherever we're going, I hope it's not far," I said while trying to spit hair out of my mouth. "I don't know how much longer I can hold on!"

"Ohhhhhhh!" Zoey wailed. "This is weird!"

"I see it!" Zander exclaimed. "I see it!"

"See what?" Zoey asked. "I still can't see anything with you on my head!"

I still couldn't see either.

It's a good thing Zander's fur was short. It didn't get in his eyes the way my hair was in my eyes. And of course, Zander had special eagle eyes that helped him see for miles and miles.

"I see the volcano," Zander said. "I see where we're going! Fire is taking us to that volcano in Hawaii. Smoke is coming out of its top!"

"Ohhhhhhh!" Zoey said again, sounding

miserable. "Ohhhhhh!"

Suddenly I could feel us slowing down. The feather wasn't pulling so hard, and the wind wasn't as loud in my ears.

Lower and lower we dropped in the sky until we were just feet from the top of the volcano's rim. Gently, we landed on the deep black sand covering the edge of the volcano.

Once we were on solid ground, Zander jumped off Zoey's shoulders. I hugged my friends. I was so happy to be standing. We all took a deep breath.

"Hey, what's that smell?" Zander asked.

I had been too scared to notice before, but now that Zander mentioned it, I wanted to plug my nose. It smelled like rotten eggs.

"Is that the volcano?" Zoey asked. Her eyes had turned a soft gray to match the smoke coming from the huge crater at the top of the volcano.

I was about to shrug, but before I could, a dark cloud of smoke puffed out of the volcano forcefully. A deep, throaty laugh came with it.

"Of course it is, my dears. Of course!"

We looked at each other. There was only one thing that voice could belong to.
The Element *Fire*.

CHAPTER 3

THE RETIREMENT PARTY

I felt my friends inch closer to me. They were probably as nervous as I was.

"Hello, Miss Fire," I said. "How are you? Is everything okay?"

Fire laughed again as another dark cloud of smoke rose. "Oh, of course, my dears, of course." Her voice was scratchy, but she sounded strong and very proper. "So glad you could make it. I thought it was high time that I formally introduced myself." More smoke rose from the volcano, but this time it was shaped like a heart. "It's so very lovely to meet you." Slowly the heart disappeared.

I looked at my friends with wide eyes. I didn't

expect Fire to make smoke hearts. That was interesting.

"It's a pleasure to make your acquaintance," I said. Then I curtsied. Fire seemed so fancy with the way she was talking. A curtsey seemed like the right thing to do.

"Now then," Fire said, "since we have introductions out of the way, let's talk about the true purpose of this meeting."

"Yes, Miss Fire," I said. "Is there anything we can do for you?"

"I have an invitation for you, my dears. You are warmly invited to the biggest show of the century, which I will be putting on shortly. The greatest, grandest eruption of Kilauea the volcano!"

Zoey shivered. I frowned. Zander growled.

"Now, I know that as soon as the explosions begin, you'll be called over here to calm me down, and I simply figured I would spare you the surprise. Clear your schedules now! Tell Air and the rest of the Elements to behave so they don't distract you. In six hours there will be fireworks in the sky above Hawaii! *Real* fireworks—volcanic fireworks! It would be lovely if you could attend the celebration."

I pushed my hair from my face and tried to

take a deep breath through my mouth so I didn't have to smell the awful rotten eggs. It was worse than when I had been sprayed by skunk smell the night before. Then I tried to think.

"Miss Fire—"

"Please, call me Flicka. I've never liked being called *Fire*. It sounds so, well, *hot*."

I looked at my friends. Zoey's eyes had darkened to match the black sand. Gray dust covered Zander's fur. They both looked back as if to say, *Is Fire crazy? Of course Fire is hot!*

"Okay, Miss Flicka," I said. "We know that Air has been going around bothering the other Elements. You don't have to put on a show just because Air dared you. I think he just says things like that because…"

I didn't know how to finish the sentence. I didn't want to say something mean about Air, but I did want to convince Fire—or Flicka—that we didn't need a big eruption.

"Oh, I'm not doing it because of silly old Air," Fire said. "I care nothing about what Air says, even if he is a rascal sometimes." She paused as another heart of smoke rose from the volcano. "I'm doing it as a way to celebrate Mother Nature's life. After all, she might not be around much longer. I want her to go out with a bang, as they say!"

I felt my heart start to beat faster. Zoey grabbed my arm tighter, and Zander growled again.

"What do you mean, Miss Flicka?" I asked. "Why won't she be around much longer?"

"Oh, of course, you already know, don't you, my dear? If Mother Nature is sick, she might need to *retire*."

"Retire?" I asked. I couldn't believe what I was hearing.

"Yes, *retire*. It might be time for Aurelia to move on and let the next Mother Nature take over."

I really didn't understand what Fire meant. Was *retire* supposed to be a code for something, somehow?

"Do you mean my sister might *die*?" I asked. My heart was beating even faster.

"Oh no, darling. Mother Natures never die. When it's time to pass on their jobs to whoever is next, they find their favorite spots in the world and go there to rest and relax. They just watch what happens with the next Mother Nature. Perhaps they even eat popcorn, like they're watching movies."

I was confused.

"And my sister is ready to retire?" I asked.

Fire laughed her throaty, scratchy laugh. Smoke from the volcano formed a circle for a moment before dissolving.

"Oh, we really can't know for sure, darling. No Mother Nature has ever been sick like this before, so we simply don't know what will happen. But I feel it is my duty to prepare for whatever may come, and don't you agree that your sister deserves a proper retirement party?"

I didn't answer. I didn't know what to say.

Zander nudged me. "If Mother Natures retire in their favorite spots, that means your mom is somewhere out there," he whispered. "And your grandma. And great grandma."

I hadn't thought about my mother since I was just a couple years old. I barely knew my mother. As soon as Aurelia and I could walk and speak, Uncle T had taken over raising us. Our mother was still around somewhere? Where?

I wasn't sure if it was okay for me to miss my mother or think about her. I was pretty sure being Mother Nature's daughter had different rules than normal.

Then again, I didn't know. My life was never really normal.

"Well, darlings," Fire said, "It's really time that

I put the finishing touches on the show. Only six hours to go! Please feel free to show yourself out. Isla's feather will take you home the way you came. And don't forget—clear your schedule so that you can come see the mighty Kilauea's beautiful, real fireworks this afternoon!"

My friends and I looked at each other. I was feeling a little sick, and my friends looked a little sick, too. Maybe it was breathing the rotten egg smell. Maybe it was Fire's crazy talk of Aurelia retiring. She was making me nervous. And confused.

I looked at the feather still in my hand. "Are you two ready?" I asked my friends.

Zoey nodded and wrapped her arms around my waist. Zander jumped into my arms.

"Let's go!" I said.

Immediately, we lifted into the sky and flew back to the castle.

CHAPTER 4

CALM, LOGICAL UNCLE T

Back at the castle, Uncle T was sitting at the black table. He was writing furiously on a clipboard.

Without looking up, he said, "So, you met Fire, I see."

"How did you know that?" I asked as we neared my uncle. I tried to look at what he was writing on the clipboard, but his hand covered the words.

"I can smell the smoke. It's in your hair and on your clothes."

I look at my green dress. It looked clean, but then I smelled the shoulder of my sleeve, and

Uncle T was right—it smelled like the volcano. I scrunched up my nose. This wasn't my favorite smell, but at least it was better than skunk.

Before I could say that aloud, Uncle T pointed to the empty chairs around the table. "Have a seat, please," he said. Then he checked his wristwatch and went back to scribbling across the clipboard.

We sat down.

"Did you find Mother Nature's special reading glasses in her purse?" he asked. He never looked up from his clipboard.

We nodded. Zoey opened Mother Nature's purse and dug through it. She pulled the glasses out and placed them on the table.

Uncle T glanced up. "Ah yes, very good. Very good," he said. "As you can probably see, I've been taking more messages for Mother Nature. Every plant and animal in the world wants to offer help." He sighed and shook his head, still writing.

"That's really nice of them, isn't it?" I asked. It seemed like a nice thing, but Uncle T's head shake and sigh made me wonder what he really thought.

Uncle T nodded. "It is nice of them, yes." He sighed again. "I'm just afraid that their ideas aren't really going to be helpful and—"

"Uncle T, is my sister going to die?" I blurted out.

Uncle T stopped writing and stared at me. He sat back in his chair and pulled his pocket watch from his shirt. After looking at it and putting it back, he said slowly, "What gave you that idea?"

All together, my friends and I said, "Fire."

Then, after a moment, I added, "Fire said that Aurelia might have to *retire* like the other Mother Natures, whatever that means. She made it sound like a big deal—like Aurelia was never coming back."

I dropped my eyes to the table and studied the reading glasses. I was a little nervous to hear what Uncle T was going to say in response.

"Fire is dramatic," Uncle T said. He went back to writing. "She's just looking for an excuse to create an explosion. That's all."

I sat forward in my chair and leaned on the table. Finally, I felt a little relief. Uncle T didn't seem worried. Maybe I didn't have to worry either. "Really?" I asked.

Uncle T shrugged. "Perhaps it is possible for Aurelia to retire, but retiring doesn't mean dying. And really, Aurelia is far too young to pass on Mother Nature's responsibilities to someone else. She's only been at it for two hundred years. She's practically still a baby in Mother Nature years."

"So we shouldn't believe Fire?" Zander asked.

Uncle T thought a moment. "We just have to remember that Fire is dramatic. She blows things out of proportion. Yes, she could be right, but it's unlikely."

"Where are the past Mother Natures?" Zoey asked.

Uncle T continued writing, but he shook his head just slightly. "I don't know. They don't tell me where they go to retire."

"So they could be anywhere? They could be all over?" I asked.

"Sure." He stopped writing and pushed the clipboard across the table. "Here. These are the latest messages from the Plant and Animal Kingdoms. I just finished getting them written down. Please take them up to your sister." He stood up and checked the clock at the end of his tie. "I have to visit the Plant Kingdom now to get the next set of messages."

As he turned to go, I called after him.

"Uncle T, wait."

He turned around.

"What would you be doing right now if Mother Nature was well? If you didn't have to take all these messages, what would you be doing?"

Uncle T almost smiled. "I'd keep busy. But this

is more important."

As he walked through the Plant Kingdom door, Zoey picked up Mother Nature's glasses and put them on.

"Let's check out these messages," she said.

There was so much to think about. Aurelia retiring—or not retiring. Past Mother Natures being all across the world. The messages that we needed to take up to Aurelia. My head felt so full that it might explode.

Faintly, I could feel something vibrating. I touched the keys on my belt.

"We'll have to wait until later to take these messages up," I said, looking at my belt. The orange key was buzzing. "It's the animals."

That meant thinking about other Mother Natures and retiring would also have to wait. That was probably good—then my head wouldn't explode any time soon.

Zoey took off the glasses and put them back in the purse. "Never a dull moment," she said.

My friends started walking toward the Animal Kingdom door. I took an extra second to look at the stack of messages for Aurelia. Part of me wanted to stay and look through them. How was I supposed to help my sister if I was always being called away?

I sighed and stood up. "Animals, here we come," I said.

"Wait," Zoey said. She pointed to my hand. "What are you going to do with the peacock feather that took us to see Fire? Flicka, I mean?"

I looked at the beautiful, lacy feather. I thought a moment, and then I stuck it in the middle of the Angel Trumpet flowers that Zoey had arranged into a beautiful vase the night before. The feather looked a little out of place with the flowers, but it made us smile.

And then, even though I knew it was time to go and not time for daydreaming, I thought about my mother. She was somewhere out there in the world, watching Aurelia do her job. Maybe she was watching me, too.

I took a deep breath and said, "Let's go!"

CHAPTER 5

LEON THE LION

The Animal Kingdom room looked exactly the same as it did the day before. Twelve enormous bubbles were bouncing slowly around a meadow. Each one had a picture of a different climate in it.

Yesterday we had gone to meet mudfish in the wetlands. I hoped that was *not* where we were going today. I already had my fill of mud for the next hundred years.

We knew what was supposed to happen. The bubble we needed was going to bounce toward us, and then we were going to jump inside. So we waited. And waited. It felt like it was taking forever for the bubble to bounce to us. But finally...

"Look!" Zander said. "There's one moving toward us. And, oh! It's a savanna! Lots of grass and lots of cool animals! Half the year it's wet, and half the year it's dry—and it's always pretty warm there. Ooh, I wonder if we're going to the African savanna!" He ran a circle around himself. Obviously, he was very excited.

Zoey and I looked at each other and then at Zander.

"How do you know all this?" I asked.

Zander laughed. It sounded like a dolphin—that's what his laugh always sounded like.

"I don't know. I just *know*!"

The savanna bubble was right in front of us. It bounced lightly on the ground.

"Ready?" I asked.

"For sure!" Zander jumped before I could say anything else, and he disappeared into the bubble.

Zoey and I looked at each other.

"He really was ready," Zoey said.

She and I held hands and counted. "One, two, three!" We closed our eyes and jumped into the bubble.

It didn't feel like anything happened—I didn't feel like I had gone anywhere. But when I opened my eyes, I definitely wasn't still in the castle.

"Yee-ha!" Zander yelled, running in circles through the tall grasses.

Zoey giggled. "Look how happy he is."

I nodded. Zander sure did love to run.

A light rain was falling. Zander had mentioned a wet season. Maybe we were at the savanna during that wet season. It was hard to tell. The tall grass all around us was brown, so maybe it hadn't been raining much. But then a couple big trees that looked like umbrellas were in the distance, and they looked pretty green. The sky was gray, like rain was on its way.

"Zander," I called. "What are we doing here? Who called us?"

From behind, I heard a growl. Then a roar.

Immediately Zoey and I grabbed onto each other. We slowly turned around.

Before us stood a big lion with a full mane. But it wasn't just any lion. It was a red lion.

Red! I hadn't ever heard of a red lion, and I definitely hadn't seen one either.

I tried to understand what was happening. I was standing five feet away from a lion.

Yikes!

And the lion was red.

Yikes again!

"Rooooooaaaar!!" Zander bellowed. He ran at

full speed toward us and the lion. "Rooooooooaaaaaar!" The sound matched the lion's roar exactly.

Why was he running at a lion? That couldn't be a good idea.

Zander! I wanted to call. *Stop, don't do that!*

But I couldn't find my voice. It had disappeared.

"Rrrrrr?" The lion said. He tilted his head to one side. "Rrrrrr?" He dropped to the ground and covered his nose with his paws.

Zander turned to Zoey and me. "Leon wants to talk to you," he said.

I opened my eyes wide. "Really?" I asked. "Leon? You mean the lion?" I looked at the lion. "I can't talk to a lion, Zander."

The lion, Leon, seemed a little less scary now that he was hiding his nose with his paws on the ground.

Zander wagged his tail. "Sure you can, Feenie. Leon is different. He's one of Mother Nature's oldest friends. He can almost speak like a person—you just have to concentrate really hard to hear him. You have enough of Mother Nature's powers to hear. I'm sure of it. Just try."

My eyes were probably still pretty wide. "You were able to find out *all that* by roaring a couple times?"

Zander turned his head to the sky and howled.

"I'm amazing!" he said.

Then he howled again.

Zoey and I giggled. Obviously Zander really liked being able to talk to animals.

I turned to Leon and closed my eyes. I listened really hard.

In my mind, I could hear a voice.

"Sarafina, you've got to help me," Leon said. "Water and Earth are driving me crazy. I can't take it anymore."

Another voiced suddenly sounded all around us as the mist got thicker.

"Leon, I don't like you saying that!"

I recognized the voice. It was the Element Water.

The ground rumbled, just slightly, and another voice filled the air.

"I don't like that either, Leon. How could you say that about us?"

And that voice was the Element Earth.

Leon shook his head and then hid his nose with his paws again. I almost thought I saw him roll his eyes.

"Oh no," he said. "Here we go again."

CHAPTER 6

ZOEY'S MAGIC

"Um, Zander?" Zoey whispered. "Is it me, or is Leon *red*?"

Leon must have heard Zoey's question. He looked out from beneath his paws. "No, it's not you. My fur is reddish. Sort of red-brown. My mother always said the red meant I was special."

I wanted to say to Leon that his mother was right. I could tell he was special. But with Water and Earth showing up, I probably needed to deal with them first.

I looked to the sky. It was still full of a warm mist.

"Miss Water? Miss Earth? How are you doing?" I asked.

I paused, waiting for them to answer. But they

didn't.

"Are you, um, having a good afternoon?" I asked.

"I most certainly am *not*!" Earth rumbled. "It's supposed to be the wet season here in that savanna, and *Water* isn't raining like she should be."

"How can you say that, Earth?!" Water gasped. "Yesterday you said I was raining too much. Now you say I'm not raining enough. All you ever do is complain about me. Complain, complain, complain."

"Yesterday we were in the desert. You aren't supposed to rain there. You're supposed to rain *here*."

Zoey, Zander, Leon, and I looked at each other. Leon shook his head and rolled his eyes.

"I don't like this arguing," Zoey said softly. She took a step backward, and then another. Slowly, she started doing turns through the tall, soft grass. She hummed quietly to herself. It was her way of blocking out Water and Earth's bickering as she twirled further and further away.

"I'm just trying to stand up for what's best here in the savanna," Earth said. "These plants and animals need more water. I have to stand up for them because if I don't, who will?"

My eyebrows furrowed. Earth's last question seemed odd to me.

"Um, Miss Earth, you know, I'm here to help, too," I said. "Don't forget about me. Maybe we can work something out."

Zander nudged Leon. "Come on, Leon. Sarafina needs to talk to Earth and Water. Let's go play. I have some questions for you about the cool stuff Mother Nature taught you to do."

Leon sighed gratefully and then stood up. Zander ran off. Leon followed him.

"Sarafina," Earth said, "We know that you're trying your best. But with Mother Nature being sick, the Elements and I really need to take care of ourselves more. What if Mother Nature doesn't get better? We can't rely on her forever."

My heart sank. There it was again: more Elements talking about Aurelia not getting better and not being around forever.

"Have you been talking to Fire?" I asked. "Because Mother Nature isn't going anywhere. I asked Uncle T about it. He said Fire was just being dramatic."

"Yes, Fire is dramatic," Water said. Mist continued to fall across the tall grasses. "But we're also worried about the future. We have to plan. Just in case."

Again my heart felt like it was sinking. "Don't you think I can help you?"

"Of course!" Water said. "But you're still learning. What about in the meantime?"

Before I could respond, Earth made a strange sound—almost like laughing.

"Oh my goodness!" Earth said, still almost laughing. "That tickles! What is this all about? Why am I being tickled?"

I looked all around. Earth was being tickled? By what? How? What was she talking about?

"Oh goodness, stop!" Earth started laughing louder and harder. "Oh, this is so strange. What's happening? *He-he-he-he-he!*"

Just then, I heard Zander running behind me.

"Sarafina!" he called, out of breath. "Look what Zoey is doing! Look what's happening!"

I whirled around. Zander was almost to my side already. In the distance, I could see where Zoey had wandered off. She was still humming and twirling, her arms waving slowly and gracefully over her head.

"Look at the grass," Zander said.

"Ohhh, stop!" Earth continued to laugh.

I saw what Zander meant. The grass was waving the same way that Zoey's arms were waving. It was like the grass was dancing *with*

Zoey.

Leon walked up behind Zander and me.

"And it's growing," the beautiful red lion said. "She's helping to make the grass grow with her singing and dancing."

I gasped and covered my mouth. So that's what Aurelia meant about Zoey's talents with singing and dancing. She could help plants grow.

"This is amazing," I said under my breath.

"It must be…" Earth said, gasping for breath, "the roots of the grasses that are…tickling me!" She continued laughing. "I've never felt anything grow so fast!"

Water sniffed. "See, Earth—maybe you didn't need any more water from me. You just needed Zoey."

"Oh, Zoey," Earth laughed, "you crazy girl, you! I didn't know you had that power!"

Zoey didn't seem to hear. She continued to dance and hum softly.

Water stopped talking, although she continued to mist. Earth stopped talking, although she continued to laugh. Zander, Leon, and I fell silent.

Leon sighed. He lay down on the grass and relaxed.

A couple minutes passed, and then Zoey twirled toward us. When she got all the way back, she smiled.

"No more arguing?" she asked. "Sarafina, did you fix the problem?"

I squeezed my friend into a hug. "No, silly, you did! Your dancing and singing helped the grass grow, which was exactly what Earth and Water needed. That's another talent you have—helping plants grow!"

Zoey smiled. Her light brown eyes—which matched the grass—grew wide. "Really?"

Zander jumped on Zoey and licked her face. "Great job, Zoe!"

We laughed.

"Come on," I said. "Let's go back to the castle."

Our work was done. I waved to Leon. The wave was also meant for Water and Earth, but I wasn't quite sure if they could see it.

To get back, we had to jump really hard, just like we wanted to pop the bubble that got us there. I grabbed Zoey's hand so we could jump together.

"Feenie?" Zander asked slowly. "Could I stay here a little while longer? I want to talk to Leon. He's the first animal I've met that can communicate with humans like me. I have some questions for him."

I smiled. "Of course. Come back to the castle whenever you want." I turned my smile toward Leon. "And Leon, your mom was right. You are special."

Leon almost looked like he was smiling back. "Thanks, *Feenie*."

CHAPTER 7

ONE BIRD, TWO BIRDS, THREE BIRDS

Zoey and I looked at each other.

Together, we said, "One, two, three!"

We jumped as hard as we could, and suddenly we were back in the Animal Kingdom wing of the castle.

"That was awesome," I said, hugging my friend again.

We walked to the White Room.

"I didn't know I was making things grow," Zoey said. "I was just trying to get away from Earth and Water arguing."

"And you made something really amazing happen."

On the black table was Uncle T's most recent stack of messages from plants and animals.

"Time to get back to the messages," I said. "Do you still have the reading glasses?"

Zoey nodded. She pulled the glasses out of Mother Nature's purse and handed them to me. We sat at the table, and I put the glasses on. Immediately, the top page on the stack of messages came to life.

It was an underwater scene. Two beautiful black-and-white striped fish with yellow streaks on their heads and tail fins swam around in circles. They seemed to be following each other. Over and over they switched directions so each one had a turn being the leader. They made fish faces at me.

"I wish I could understand them," I said. "I wish Zander was here. We can't really do much without him, can we?"

Zoey was quiet while she thought. "Maybe try flipping to a page with just plants. I might be able to understand the message."

"Good idea." I took off the glasses and handed them to Zoey. Then I handed the stack of notes to her. "Go ahead and take a look. Hopefully you can hear something."

I watched my friend put the glasses on and flip through the pages slowly. With each one she flipped, she shook her head and said softly, "no, not this one…not this one…no, not this one."

I crossed my fingers under the table.

Coo! Coo! Coo!

Where was that sound coming from? I looked around. Had I just heard some birds? That couldn't have been possible. There weren't any birds in the White Room. And only the person wearing Mother Nature's glasses could hear the messages in Uncle T's notes—so it couldn't be that either.

Coo! Coo! Coo!

I looked around again. That sound—it was so familiar. I looked at Zoey. She didn't seem to notice it. She was still looking carefully at the messages.

Coo! Coo!

I looked up and gasped. There, at the top of the ceiling were two white doves. They weren't in Aurelia's room, which was magically hidden somewhere beyond the ceiling. They were actually *in* the castle, flying around as though they had gotten out of Aurelia's room.

"Zoey, look!" I grabbed my fairy-friend's arm gently and pointed upward. Zoey took off Mother Nature's glasses. Her mouth dropped open.

"Where did they come from?" she asked.

Coo! Coo! Coo!

"We have to get Zander back," I said. "We have to find him so that he can tell us what's happening. These doves must need something. They wouldn't have come otherwise."

Just then, the Animal Kingdom door burst open and Zander came trouncing through.

"Did someone call my name?" he said in a singsong voice. "I'm here, at your service! And boy do I have a surprise for you!"

"We have a surprise for you, too," I said. I pointed upward. "Look, somehow the doves got in here."

Zander laughed his dolphin laugh. "Wow, how did they do that?"

"We don't know," Zoey said. "We were hoping you could find out for us."

"Perfect. That will be a great way for me to show you my surprise."

Zander crouched down like he was about to take off running, and he closed his eyes tightly.

"Yee-ha!" he said. And with that, he leapt into the air. A second after his paws left the ground, he turned into a dove and flew upward toward the other birds.

Zoey and I gasped. We grabbed onto each other, our mouths hanging open. Then we looked at each other.

Did that really just happen? Did Zander just turn into a bird?

I blinked hard. When I opened my eyes again, I looked toward the ceiling. Just as I had seen a second before, there were now three birds flying together.

And one of them was Zander.

"No way," I breathed.

CHAPTER 8

MELTDOWN

Zoey squeezed my arm and shook it a little. "What! Is! Happening!? Am I seeing things?"

I shook my head. "No," I said slowly.

I blinked hard. Then I blinked again.

I said, "When you dance, the plants grown. And now Zander can turn into a bird. This is crazy."

Just at that moment, Uncle T threw open the Plant Kingdom door and walked briskly toward me and Zoey. Uncle T always did things in a hurry, but this was different. Normally he seemed quick but calm. This time, he didn't look calm. His eyes were wide and serious.

With his clipboard tucked under one arm, he pointed his free hand toward the ceiling. "Why are there birds in here? How did they get in here?"

Somehow, I felt like I was in trouble. Did I do something wrong? I didn't *think* so.

Gulp.

"Well, Uncle T, one of the birds is Zander," I said. "He somehow jumped and turned into a bird."

Uncle T didn't seem surprised by this, so I continued.

"And as for the other two birds," I shrugged, "I don't know."

"Did they come from outside?" Uncle T pointed to a wall behind us, but we knew he meant what was on the other side of the wall. "Or did they come from Mother Nature's room?" He pointed to the ceiling where Aurelia's room was hidden.

I shrugged again. "I'm not sure," I said. "We didn't see them come from outside."

Zoey was hiding behind me just a little. She poked her head out and said softly, "They didn't come from outside. We would have seen them. They weren't here when we came back, so they must have come down from Mother Nature's room."

Uncle T still did not look happy.

Something above caught my attention. I looked up. One of the white doves was swooping down toward us. It landed on the ground at our feet and then turned into a dog.

"Zander!" Zoey and I exclaimed. We bent down and hugged our doggy friend's neck.

"How did you do that?" Zoey asked.

Zander wagged his tail excitedly.

"I just had a feeling," Zander said. "Yesterday when my nose started glowing like a firefly, I knew there was something going on. Mother Nature had said there was something special about me, and I thought the firefly nose was a sign. That's why I stayed behind to talk to Leon. I thought he might be able to help me understand my talents. And guess what? He *did*!"

"Zander," Uncle T said. "What did the doves say? Why are they here?"

Uncle T didn't seem as excited about Zander's new talent as we were.

Zander's tongue hung out the side of his mouth. He was breathing hard. It must have been from learning to fly.

"Mother Nature is getting worse," he said. "The doves were worried. They didn't know what to do."

"They broke through Mother Nature's room," Uncle T said. He shook his head. "That's really bad. If the animals can break through her room, it means that she's getting weak. Her powers are losing strength. No one and no animal should be able to go in and out of the castle without permission, and that includes Aurelia's room."

I looked at Uncle T with scared eyes. "What do we do? What *can* we do?" I asked.

Uncle T didn't answer. He looked toward the ceiling, thinking. I expected him to check his watch since he did that just about every twenty seconds, but he didn't. He must have been really distracted by this.

"Zander, should we go see her?" I asked. "Does she need us to go see her?"

Uncle T answered before Zander could. "Unless you have a cure, it won't matter. Just seeing her won't help her. And it will only upset you or make you sad."

I looked at my friends. My heart felt like it was going to burst through my chest from worrying. Zoey hugged my arm, and Zander nuzzled my legs.

My belt vibrated.

I grabbed my key ring and looked at it.

I said, "Oh no. Fire is calling us."

Zoey gulped. "Does that mean she's making the volcano have that huge eruption?"

"Ugh," Uncle T said, rolling his eyes. "Of course! *Of course* Fire is doing that *right now*. Of all times, she picks right now to create a big scene."

I had never seen Uncle T seem so frustrated before. I didn't know what to think.

Uncle T continued, "With so much else going on, this silly volcano really could have waited. I was hoping the Elements would have enough respect for Mother Nature to settle down a little while she was sick, but I guess I was foolish in thinking that." He threw his hands in the air. "Oh, just go to Fire, you three. Go and get her under control."

We looked at each other. We didn't move.

"Uncle T," I said gently, "you seem a little tired. Maybe you need to take a break. Can we get you something to help you rest?"

Uncle T took a deep breath. Then another.

"I'm sorry. I didn't mean to get upset." He paused and took another deep breath. "I'm fine. Just go take care of Fire."

We didn't move.

"We're here to help each other," I said. "Even you. We stick together like family."

Uncle T nodded. "The whole world is family—the

plants, the animals, the humans—we're all in this together." He paused. "Thank you for keeping everything together. Including me. Now go!"

CHAPTER 9

KNOCK, KNOCK

The trip to Fire was less wild this time. Sure, we flew there using one of Isla's fallen tail feathers again, but this time, we knew what to expect. I held the feather with one hand and linked arms with Zoey. Zander turned into a white dove and rode on my shoulder.

As we flew through the air to Kilauea, I could see that the smoke was much thicker and darker than it had been the last time. The smell of rotten eggs was even stronger.

"Where should we go exactly?" Zoey asked.

We were slowing down and flying lower.

I thought for a moment. Zoey had a good

question.

"I don't know if we should land," I said. "We don't want to be too close when the volcano erupts."

Before I could say anything else, Fire's voice rose from the volcano.

"Welcome to the show, darlings!" she said with a low, throaty laugh. The smoke coming out of the volcano curled into a smiley face. "Oh, do please stay in the air. Tell Isla's feather not to drop you off. I want you to have a good view, but safety first. Anywhere in the air will work quite nicely, I'm sure. Really, there isn't a bad seat in the house!"

"Feenie," Zander-the-bird said softly, "I don't know if you should try to talk her out of this."

Not talk Fire out of the big eruption? I couldn't believe what I was hearing. What was Zander thinking?

"What do you mean?" I whispered.

"There isn't going to be time. You can't be nice and try to change her mind. You just have to stop her, whether she likes it or not."

I could see Zander's point. Talking an Element out of an idea took time. This volcano was going to blow up soon—there wasn't time to talk Fire out of her original plan.

But wouldn't that make Fire just get madder? And then what would happen?

"I agree, Feenie," Zoey said. "She's made up her mind, and we won't be able to reason with her. We just have to stop her."

"But how?"

Really, how does someone stop Fire?!? It's Fire!

"Use your powers," both my friends said in a loud whisper.

"Concentrate!" Zoey added.

"Would anyone like a refreshment before the show?" Fire asked. "I've got hot lava pie and fiery fireballs. I can serve them up straight away!"

"Um, no thank you Miss Flicka," I said. I spoke slowly. I was trying to stall and think of a plan.

My friends were right. There wasn't time to change Fire's mind. But I didn't know if I *could* concentrate enough to stop her. So far, most of the times I'd tried to fix a problem I'd ended up making it into a bigger problem. Mixed up rainbows, rain falling to the sky instead of the ground, bouncy islands...

"Feenie, you just have to believe," Zander said.

"*We* believe you can do it," Zoey added.

"How about a refreshing beverage?" Fire

asked. "I've got spicy molten mochas coming right up!"

"Um," I said, still talking slowly and trying to figure out what to do. "That sounds lovely, but we're not thirsty just now. Perhaps a little later. Thank you."

We continued flying in circles above the volcano. The smoke was getting thicker and thicker. We were trying to stay away from it, but Alya's feather was really the one in charge. We had to go where she took us. Luckily, the feather seemed like it wanted to stay away from the smoke, too.

Wait! I thought. *I have it! An idea!*

"Hey, Miss Flicka?" I said. "You've worked so hard putting this show together. How about me and my friends get you all warmed up for the big event with a little comedy? Maybe we could give you a moment to relax before the big event."

"Comedy?" Fire asked. The smoke from the volcano swirled into a heart. "I love comedy. Yes, I think a couple jokes before the show would be quite nice. Very relaxing."

"What are you doing?" Zander hissed. And it really was a hiss—he was a bird who suddenly sounded like a snake. "Comedy?"

"We're not funny!" Zoey whispered loudly.

I knew my friends were right, but I had to try something. Bravely, I said, "Knock, knock!"

Fire laughed. "Oh, how I love knock-knock jokes. Good choice for an opener, Sarafina. *Who's there?*" she sang.

I didn't answer right away. *Yikes!* I hadn't figured out the rest of the joke yet.

"Fire!" I blurted out.

"Fire who?" Fire asked.

Again, I didn't answer right away.

"Um, fire that girl who can't stand the heat!"

Fire didn't respond. The smoke coming from the volcano thinned a little bit, like Fire had paused it while she thought.

"Well, Miss Sarafina," Fire sniffed, "that wasn't very funny. Maybe I should fire *you* from making jokes as part of the opening act!"

"Feenie, no more jokes," Zander whispered. His voice was back to normal.

"Yes, just stop her," Zoey added. "You're going to make her mad!"

"I've got a plan," I whispered back to them. Then louder, I said, "Miss Flicka, sorry about that. I know that wasn't a good one. I've got a better one. Give me one more try."

Fire took her time to think about my request. Then she said, "All right. Continue."

I started concentrating as hard as I could. In my mind, I commanded, *stop the eruption, make the lava sink back into the volcano. Stop the eruption, don't let the lava bubble over."*

Out loud, I said, "Knock, knock!"

In my head, I thought really hard. *Lava sink back. Don't bubble over. Lava sink back. Don't bubble over.*

"Who's there?" Fire sang.

Lava sink back. Don't bubble over.

"Sarafina, *who's there?"* Fire repeated.

Lava sink back. Don't bubble over.

"Fire's special!" I blurted out.

"Fire's special who?" Fire asked.

Lava sink back. Don't bubble over.

"Fire's special magic trick!"

And then it happened. Suddenly, the heat coming from the volcano weakened. The smoke started getting lighter and thinner.

"Sarafina, what did you do?" Zoey whispered.

"I wanted to make Fire think she did a magic trick by making the lava all disappear," I whispered back. "I think it might have worked. Look! The volcano is calming down. We just have to convince her that she did magic!"

"Do you think that was a good idea?" Zander asked. "I really don't understand. What do you mean?"

I looked at my bird friend sitting on my shoulder. I *had* thought it was a good idea. But now that Zander seemed doubtful, I wondered if I hadn't really had a good idea at all. It had made sense in my head. Maybe it didn't make sense out loud.

Uh-oh, I thought.

"What is going on!?" Fire thundered. "What happened to the lava!?"

"You did a magic trick!" I said. "Look at this amazing feat!" I was trying to sound confident, but I did *not* feel confident. Not at all. This wasn't a good idea.

Drat!

"I most certainly did *not* do *this!*" Fire said.

And then, suddenly, I understood what Fire really meant.

Pink bubbles began rising from the volcano. All sizes, all shapes. Pink bubbles everywhere. The volcano was erupting bubbles. Real bubbles.

I think my heart might have stopped beating for a moment.

I had made a mistake again. I must not have been clear enough with my concentration. I had wanted the lava to *sink* back. I wanted it to stop from *bubbling* over. I didn't want *pink bubbles*!

I smiled.

"That's fantastic! I'm glad to hear that because I can't understand anything they're saying."

I kept smiling. I was getting used to relying on my friends to help with Mother Nature's jobs. They could do so much that I couldn't when it came to plants and animals.

"Put the glasses on me," Zander said. "Watch!"

I did as Zander asked. I had never seen a Golden Retriever wear glasses before. It was quite a snazzy fashion statement.

"See, let me tell you what these monkeys are saying—" Zander began.

But before he could finish his sentence, something on my belt buzzed.

"Oh!" I yelped.

It was the key ring that I kept with me all the time. The keys vibrated whenever there was a Mother Nature job to do.

My heart sank. I wanted to find out what the monkeys were saying.

"Who is it?" Zoey asked. She could see me looking at the keys on my belt.

Eek! I thought once I saw which key was vibrating. It was red.

"Fire." I winced. "It's the Element Fire."

One of my jobs filling in for Mother Nature was to help control the four Elements: Air, Water, Earth, and Fire. So far, we had gotten to know a little bit about three of them. Air was rascally. Water was weepy. Earth was happy as long as none of the other Elements bothered her.

We hadn't met Fire yet. I had been worried about this one.

Fire, I said to myself. *Hot, burning, wild fire.*

Yikes.

Zander put his head to the ground and let the glasses slip off his face. "Let's do this," he said. "Time to go meet Fire!"

I took a deep breath and nodded. Zander was right. We couldn't put it off any longer.

CHAPTER 10

PINK BUBBLES

"Feenie," Zoey whispered, "this is definitely safer than lava—good idea about that. But, um," she paused, "I think this might make Fire even madder."

Zander snapped his mouth, trying to catch the bubbles floating by.

"This is awesome!" he said. "I love bubbles. Quick, get Isla's feather to start following the bubbles around. I want to catch some."

"Zander!" Zoey exclaimed. "This is no time to catch bubbles. We need to focus. Plus, you're not even a dog right now. Birds don't like to snap at bubbles!"

"Oh no, oh no," I said under my breath. The pink bubbles continued to float out of the volcano, slowly lifting higher and higher into the air. As we flew around the bubbles, I noticed the rotten eggs smell wasn't as strong. At least that awful smell was going away. I was trying to look on the bright side, after all.

"Sarafina!" Fire yelled. "Sara*fina!*"

And then another sound whooshed by us—a familiar sound.

"Oh *Feenie!*" the voice said. "You did it again!"

I knew exactly who was talking. It was the Element Air. *Of course* he had to show up right now.

"I don't have long to chat," Air continued. "I just wanted to pop by and say *bravo*. No, really, *bravo*. The whole world is going to love seeing Kilauea erupting pink bubbles. Beautiful. Just lovely."

"Air!" Zander growled, just like a dog in a bird's body.

A gust of wind swooshed by.

"Gotta jet," Air said. "Ta-ta for now!"

And with another swooshing wind, Air was gone.

I could feel my heartbeat going a mile a minute. My face was feeling hot from the inside.

My whole body was shaking. This was bad. So, so bad.

"Sarafina!" Fire said again. "Sarafina!" She was sputtering, like she couldn't think of anything else to say but my name. "Sarafina!"

And then, a huge burst of pink bubbles exploded from the top of the volcano. And it was followed by...

By...

By the sound of Fire's laughter.

"I can't believe what just happened!" she said. "How did you know pink is my favorite color? I've been stuck with red all my life, and I've always just wanted to tone it down to a nice, soft pink. In fact, I've often wondered if people would take more kindly to me if I were pink—a lovely shade of pink."

"Pink would be stunning," Zoey said, thinking quickly. "But you know, all the great shades of color that you are—red, orange, even blue—those are beautiful, too. I've always wanted my eyes to match the beautiful whitish-blue that you have."

Another burst of bubbles erupted.

"My, that's so flattering," Fire said.

An idea crashed through my mind. It hit me like a flash. I didn't know if it would work—or if it would be allowed, but I had to try.

"Miss Flicka, maybe this one time we can make your lava pink. Maybe a little red still, but mostly pink. How would you like that?"

The bubbles continued floating upward at a steady pace as fire thought about my suggestion.

And then, she said, "Hmm. What do you mean?"

"We can change the bubbles back into lava, but keep the pink color. I just think that if we do it, we should make the lava move nice and slowly. That way, there's plenty of time to admire the beautiful color."

I really just wanted the eruption to be safer, but I wasn't going to tell Fire *that*.

Again, Fire didn't answer right away. The bubbles continued flowing upward steadily. We continued flying in circles around them.

"Hmm," she finally said. "That might be even better than the big extravaganza I was planning. Pink*ish* lava. Hmm. Yes, I like that. Let's give it a whirl, Sarafina!"

Zoey squeezed my arm happily. Zander snapped at a couple more bubbles and laughed like a dolphin.

This time, I knew I could do it. Now that the pressure of acting fast was gone, I could concentrate the way I needed to. I definitely could get those bubbles to turn into pink lava. I closed my eyes.

Lava, I thought. *Pink lava. Pink lava. Pink lava.*

I opened my eyes.

The bubbles began to thin out. Fewer and fewer came out of the volcano. My friends and I held our breath, waiting. What was going to happen when the bubbles were all gone? Was *anything* going to happen?

"A-ha!" Fire laughed. "My goodness, that certainly is a lovely shade of pink. Brilliant. Just brilliant!"

And a moment later, we saw it. Dark pink lava began oozing out of the volcano, nice and slowly.

I thought the color was just barely pink. To people who weren't focusing on the exact shade, they might not have even noticed since it was nearly red. But clearly Fire thought it was pink, and that's all that mattered.

"Thank you, Sarafina, for this top-notch idea," Fire said. "It's truly a delight." She paused and sighed. "I just wish that Mother Nature was around to see it."

"What do you mean?" I asked. Suddenly, I was worried again. "Do you mean something *else* happened to my sister? Something else since we saw you this afternoon?"

The Elements always seemed to know what was happening before I did. I was hoping this wasn't the case right now. I waited for Fire to answer. And waited. And waited.

Was she waiting to make me even more nervous than I already was?

Uncle T *did* say she was dramatic.

CHAPTER 11

THE GRANDMOTHERS OF NATURE

"Oh no, Sarafina," Fire said. "She's no worse off than she was before, but she is still doing very poorly. My goodness, don't you just love the sight of pink lava? It truly takes my breath away. *Truly.*"

The rotten eggs smell had returned, and I wanted to fly back to the castle. I had to get back to my sister. Time to figure out a friendly way to say goodbye.

I nodded. "Oh yes, it is beautiful."

"But I was thinking, darling, about Mother Nature." Fire paused. "You know, I am by far the smartest of the four Elements, and certainly the hardest working. You'll always get the best ideas from me, and like I was saying, I've been thinking about how Mother Nature has been so sick."

I couldn't help but scrunch my eyebrows. Sure Fire was smart, but so were the other Elements. I didn't want to disagree with her, though, especially if she was going to say something to help cure my sister.

"Earth's plants and animals have been sending you all sorts of useless ideas, and Water's plants and animals have been doing the same. *All useless.* Then there is Air, who doesn't even bother trying to be helpful. He's just a nuisance." She sighed dramatically. "But me, *I* want to help."

We stopped circling the volcano. Isla's feather held us in one place—as though it was now paying attention to Fire's words and didn't want to miss anything.

"Um," I said, "Thank you?"

"Oh, you are quite welcome, dear. Quite welcome. You know, everyone and everything is looking in the wrong places to help Mother Nature. To help her, you should seek the wisest advice there is."

"Miss Flicka, who has the wisest advice?" I asked.

"Why, past Mother Natures, of course."

My eyebrows scrunched again. Past Mother

Natures? What was Fire talking about?

"Oh, I've confused you, haven't I?" Fire asked. "You're still new on the job. Let me explain a moment before I rest for the evening. All this flowing has worn me out, and I would like to relax and enjoy the sights for awhile." She paused and thought a moment. "Go to the four corners of the Earth where the Grandmothers of Nature are. Ask their help. They know far more than any plant, animal, or Element."

"How do we do that?" I asked.

"Oh, Sarafina," Fire said slowly with a soft laugh. "I may be smart, but I don't know everything. Ask your uncle. Perhaps he would know. And now, if you'll excuse me, I'd like to enjoy my pink brilliance!"

I nodded. "Thank you, Miss Flicka."

I looked at my friends. There was no time to waste—and we could talk about the crazy conversation back at the castle. It was time get out of there.

"Take us home!" I commanded Isla's feather.

CHAPTER 12

A NEW JOURNEY

Once back in the castle, my friends and I barreled through Isla's throne room to the White Room. Zander had turned back into a dog. Uncle T sat at the table, furiously scribbling across the page.

"Uncle T! Uncle T!" I exclaimed breathlessly. I barely slowed down before banging into the table where he sat.

Uncle T looked up and raised an eyebrow. "Really, Sarafina? Pink lava? We're already getting reports of the strange volcano lava sighted by humans."

I shook my head. "It's the best I could do.

And it was worth it. Fire and I are friends now, and she gave me an idea about curing Aurelia!"

Uncle T sat back in his chair and checked his watch. "What's the idea?"

"We need to go to the four corners of the world and talk to the past Mother Natures. Fire called them the Grandmothers of Nature. They know everything. They'll have the answers."

Uncle T nodded slowly, considering the idea. "They do know everything. You are right. But the current Mother Nature is not allowed to see the past ones. That's just not possible. If they contact each other, who knows what will happen? Past Mother Natures might end up commanding animals and plants to do something when they don't mean to. The Elements might not know who to listen to. It could cause a lot of confusion."

My heart sank. What Uncle T said made a lot of sense. It *could* be confusing.

Out of the corner of my eye, I saw Zoey and Zander looking at each other. And then, at the same time, they both exclaimed, "But she's not Mother Nature!"

Uncle T's eyes widened. He sat forward. "You're right," he said softly. "Sarafina is *not* Mother Nature." He tapped his pen on the

JEN CARTER

clipboard, thinking. "This might actually work. No Mother Nature ever had a twin sister before you and Aurelia, and so maybe the rules are a little different for you."

I smiled, first just a little, and then a lot. I hugged my friends. Fire thought she was so smart, but she was no match for Zoey and Zander.

"So what do we do?" Zoey asked.

"Where do we go?" Zander asked.

Uncle T stood up and started pacing.

Under his breath, he began talking, thinking out loud. "The four corners of the Earth, you say. Hmm. Yes, I think visiting those four Grandmothers of Nature should get us some answers. You'll need Aurelia's purse, for sure. You'll need a map, too. Perhaps Air can give you a ride to all the places you need to visit. Zander and Zoey, you'll need to keep your powers sharp to communicate with anything you come into contact with." He stopped pacing and turned to look at the three of us. "Are you up to the task? Can you do it?"

My friends and I all nodded.

"Good. And you'll need one more thing."

We waited for Uncle T to continue.

"You need to go visit Aurelia right now," he said, pointing to the ceiling of the castle. "Go say

276

goodbye and check on her. Two more doves came through her room to the castle while you were gone—and her powers are getting weaker."

Again we nodded.

"We'll go right now," I said.

We quickly turned the black table into an elevator and zoomed up to Mother Nature's room.

There, my friends and I found Aurelia asleep under a tree. She looked exactly the same. Her eyes had purple circles around them. Her face was pale. She had a blanket made of flowers pulled across her lap, and there were two white rabbits sitting next to her, one on each side. Her hands were resting on the rabbits' backs as though they were arm rests that were there to help keep her comfortable.

I normally wouldn't want to wake my sister, but there was no choice. I walked toward the tree where Aurelia was resting. My two friends followed behind.

"Aurelia" I whispered, "we've come to say goodbye. We're going on a trip to help find a cure for you."

My sister opened her eyes, just barely. She nodded. "Thank you," she said. "That's so kind of you." She closed her eyes again.

I wanted to ask Aurelia how she was feeling,

but I could already tell. She wasn't doing well at all. She seemed more tired and weak than ever before.

My friends and I looked at each other. *What else should I say?* I wanted to ask them.

But before they could answer, Aurelia spoke again.

"Is there anything you need to help with your journey?"

I thought a moment. "I think I have everything I need," I said slowly. "I think Uncle T is helping us with all that."

Together, Zoey and Zander whispered, "A map!"

My eyes grew. "Oh, yes," I said. "Uncle T mentioned a map. Do you have a map we can use?" I didn't mention what kind of map because Uncle T didn't say. I hoped she knew what he meant.

Aurelia took a deep breath. Slowly, softy, she said, "All you need is the sun, the moon, and the stars." She took another breath. "The Elements will help you. Just ask."

My friends and I looked at each other and nodded.

"I love you, Aurelia," I said.

She nodded. "I love you, too."

With that, my friends and I stepped back onto the black platform elevator and sunk to the White Room below.

Uncle T was pacing back and forth, waiting for us to join him on the ground.

"Are you ready?" he asked.

I nodded. "Aurelia said that we don't need a map. She said that the sun, the stars, and the moon are all that we'll need."

"And then the Elements will help you?" Uncle T asked.

"Yes, exactly."

Uncle T nodded. "Well then," he said, "time to get started."

He walked toward Isla's throne room. At the door, he turned and looked at us. "Ask Air for a meeting. He can give you a ride wherever you need to go."

I looked at Isla's door and thought a moment.

"How long do you think we have?" I asked. "How much longer do we have to find a cure?"

Uncle T pursed his lips. "Just get back here as soon as you can."

I nodded. And then, without thinking, I threw myself at Uncle T, hugging him as tightly as I could. I hadn't ever hugged Uncle T—not as far as I could remember—but I couldn't help myself.

He patted me on the back.

"You're a good girl, Sarafina," he said. "And you've got fantastic friends. You can do this."

I let go of my uncle and forced a smile at my friends.

"Let's go," I said.

And with that, the three of us walked through the door to Isla's throne room.

The Sarafina Series by Jen Carter

Sarafina and the Mixed up Rainbow (#1)
Sarafina and the Muddy Mess (#2)
Sarafina and the Bouncy Island (#3)
Sarafina and the Bubbly Volcano (#4)
Sarafina and the Protected Pyramid (#5)
Sarafina and the Protected Pyramid (#5)
Sarafina and the Bamboozled Countryside (#6)
Sarafina and the Raging Rainforest (#7)
Sarafina and the Broken Rules (#8)

Also by Jen Carter

Chasing Paris (New Adult Fiction)
Remembering Summer (New Adult Fiction)

ABOUT THE AUTHOR

Jen Carter grew up writing stories. The *Sarafina* series is the first set of stories inspired by Jen's daughters: one who would love to be a flower fairy and one who would love to be a Golden Retriever. She lives with her family in San Diego, California.

ABOUT THE ILLUSTRATOR

Cindy Carter is an artist, photographer, and crafter. She draws inspiration from her travels, nature, and beauty of everyday objects.

Proof

Made in the USA
Charleston, SC
20 May 2016